Donald Lam Has A Way With Women

The brunette flung herself into his arms. She pressed her face close to his. He kissed her hard. "Don't be so damned platonic," she said. . . .

But even the busiest lady's man has to take time out for trouble. Particularly when the brunette he's been playing around with gets too chummy with a corpse. And the cops are out for blood —his blood.

ERLE STANLEY GARDNER

WRITING UNDER THE NAME

A. A. FAIR

GIVE 'EM THE

A DELL MYSTERY

Published by
DELL PUBLISHING CO., INC.
750 Third Avenue
New York 17, N.Y.

Reprinted by arrangement with
William Morrow & Company, Inc.
New York, N.Y.

Previous Dell Edition #D213

New Dell Edition
First printing—October, 1962
Second printing—January, 1963

Printed in U.S.A.

Chapter One

HOME WRECKER

As I GOT OFF THE ELEVATOR and started down the corridor, the old familiar surroundings took me back to that first day when I'd made that same journey, looking for a job.

At that time, the sign on the door had read, *B. Cool, Confidential Investigations*. Now, in 1944, it read, *Cool & Lam*, with the name *B. Cool* in one corner, and *Donald Lam* down in the other. There was something reassuring about seeing my name on the door. It was as though I really had something to come back to.

I pushed open the door.

Elsie Brand was pounding the keyboard of the typewriter. She turned and looked up over her shoulder, her face automatically assuming the welcoming smile with which one reassures the nervous clients who call to see a private detective.

I saw the expression jerk off her face. Her eyes widened.

"Donald!"

"Hello, Elsie."

"Donald! My, I'm glad to see you. *Where* did you come from?"

"South Seas, and various places."

"How long are you— When do you have to go back?"

"I don't."

"Not ever?"

"Probably not. I'm supposed to have a check-up in six months."

"What happened?"

"Bugs—tropical bugs. Okay if I take it easy for a while, live in a cool climate, and don't get too excited. Bertha in there?"

I jerked my head toward the door of the office that had *B. Cool, Private* lettered on the door.

Elsie nodded.

"How is she?"

"Same as ever."

"How's her weight?"

"Still keeping it at one hundred sixty-five, and hard as barbed wire."

"Making any money?"

"She did for a while, and then she got in sort of a rut. Things haven't been coming so well lately. Guess you'd better ask her about that."

"Have you been sitting there hammering that typewriter all the time I've been gone?"

She laughed. "No, of course not."

"What do you mean?"

"Only eight hours a day."

"Seems like pretty much of a rut to get into. I thought you'd have quit the job and gone into an airplane factory."

"Didn't you get my letters?"

"They didn't say anything about staying on the job."

"I didn't think I *had* to say anything."

"Why?"

She avoided my eyes. "I don't know. Guess it's my contribution to the war effort."

"Loyalty to the job?"

"Not to the job," she said, "so much as— Oh, I don't know, Donald. You were out there fighting and—well, I wanted to do what I could to hold the business together."

The inner office buzzer made noise.

Elsie picked up the receiver on the telephone, switched it over to Bertha Cool's office, said, "Yes, Mrs. Cool."

Bertha was so mad the receiver couldn't contain all of her voice. I could hear the rasping, angry tones over where I was sitting. "Elsie, I've told you to talk with clients only long enough to find out what they want, then call me. I'll do the talking for the outfit."

"This isn't a client, Mrs. Cool."

"Who is it?"

"A—a friend."

Bertha's voice rose a full octave. "My God! Do I pay you to hold social soirées in the office, or do I pay you to get out a little work once in a while? For God's sake—a friend! ... A ... Well, I'll soon fix that!"

The slam of the receiver in Bertha's office threatened to pull the telephone out by the roots. We heard the pound of two quick steps, then the door was jerked open and Bertha stood on the threshold, her glittering little eyes sharp with anger, her big jaw thrust out.

She flashed a swift look to get my bearings, then came barging down on me like a battleship trying to ram a submarine.

Halfway there, her eyes managed to get the message to her angry brain.

"Why, you little devil!" she said, stopping as though her feet had frozen to the floor.

For a moment she was glad to see me, then you could see her catch herself. She certainly wouldn't let anyone know it. She whirled to Elsie and said, "Why the hell didn't you tell me?"

Elsie said demurely, "I was trying to, Mrs. Cool, when you hung up. I was going to tell you that—"

"Humph!" Bertha snorted her into silence. She turned to me. "It's a wonder you wouldn't send a wire."

I used the only argument that would impress itself on Bertha's mind. "Wires cost money."

Even that didn't dent her. "Well, you could have sent one of those tourist messages. You get a low rate on those. You come busting in here and—"

Bertha broke off, her eyes on the frosted glass panel of the corridor door.

The head and shoulders of a feminine figure were silhouetted against the glass, a chic, slender woman, evidently young, and either because it was a mannerism or because of the way she was standing, the head was perked slightly to one side, giving it a jaunty appearance.

Bertha muttered, "Damn it! Clients always *do* catch me in the outer office. It's undignified. Looks as though we weren't busy."

She grabbed up a bunch of papers from Elsie's desk, struck a businesslike pose, started pawing through the papers.

But the visitor didn't come in.

There was a long matter of seconds which seemed minutes during which the silhouette was pasted against the frosted glass, then abruptly the shadow went on down the hall.

Bertha Cool slammed the papers down on the desk. "There you are," she said. "That's the way things have been going lately. The damned little tramp will probably go on down the hall to the Transcontinental Detective Agency and spill her troubles there."

I said, "Cheer up, Bertha. Perhaps she's just nervous and is coming back."

"Well," Bertha snorted, "something about the place didn't seem right to her. She was all set to come in, and then she didn't come. It didn't sound like a business office. Elsie, you start pounding that typewriter. Donald you come in the private office. Remember, Elsie, if she comes in she'll be nervous. That type won't wait. She'll sit down for a minute, then pretend she's forgotten something and jump up and run out, and that'll be the last we ever see of her. She's wearing a little hat on one side of her head with a—"

"I got a good look at her silhouette," Elsie said.

"All right. The minute she comes in let me know. Don't stall around. Reach for the telephone. After all, I can't go out in the corridor and grab 'em the way they do when a customer stops in front of a pawnshop. Indecision. Never could understand it myself. If you're going to do a thing, why not do it? Why start and stop and back and fill and mince around? Donald, come inside. Let Elsie get to work on that typewriter."

Elsie Brand flashed a glance at me and let me see the quiet amusement in her eyes, then she was pounding away again at the typewriter.

Bertha Cool put her big strong hand under my arm and said, "Come on, Donald, get in the office and tell me what this is all about."

We entered Bertha Cool's private office. Bertha strode around the desk and slammed herself down in a creaking swivel chair. I sat on the arm of a big overstuffed chair.

Bertha looked me over, said, "You've toughened up, Donald."

"I've been toughened."

"What do you weigh now?"

"A hundred and thirty-five."

"You look taller."

"I'm not taller. It's the way they made me stand."

There was a moment's silence. Bertha had an ear cocked for noises in the outer office but there was no cessation in the pounding of Elsie Brand's typewriter.

"Business not go good?" I asked.

"Terrible!" Bertha grunted.

"What's the matter with it?"

"Damned if I know. Before you came along, I was making a living piddling along with a lot of picayunish cases, little shadowing jobs, divorce cases, stuff of that sort. Mostly I got my business by catering to the domestic relations work that other agencies wouldn't handle. Then *you* came along. First rattle out of the box you threw me into the big time—more money, more risk, more excitement, more clients—and then you enlisted in the Navy and for a while I carried on all right. Then something happened. I haven't had a worthwhile case in the last year."

"What's the matter? Don't people come in any more?"

"They come in," Bertha said, "but somehow I don't impress them. They don't do things my way, and I can't do them your way. I'm sort of a hybrid."

"What do you mean, you can't do them my way?"

"Look at that chair you're sitting on," she said. "That's a good example."

"What do you mean?"

"After you became a partner you went down and spent a hundred and twenty-five dollars on that chair. Your theory was that you can't win a client's confidence when he's uneasy, and that you can't get a person to confide in you when he's uncomfortable. You let the client sit down in the depths of that chair, and it's as though he was sitting on top of the world in a feather bed. He settles back and relaxes, and starts talking."

"Well, doesn't he?"

"He seems to do it for you, but he doesn't do it for me."

I said, "Perhaps you don't make the people *feel* comfortable."

Bertha's eyes glittered angrily. "Why the hell should I? We paid a hundred and twenty-five bucks for the chair to do that. If you think I'm going to squander a hundred and twenty-five dollars just in order to—"

She broke off in midsentence.

I listened, and for a moment couldn't hear anything. Then I realized that Elsie Brand had quit typing.

A moment later the buzzer sounded on Bertha Cool's phone.

Bertha snatched the receiver off the cradle, said cautiously, "Yes?" then in a low voice, "is that the woman who . . . Oh, it is? . . . What's her name? . . . All right, send her in."

Bertha hung up the telephone and said, "Get out of that chair. She's coming in."

"Who?"

"Her name's Miss Georgia Rushe. She's coming in. She—"

Elsie Brand opened the door and said as though granting a great concession, "Mrs. Cool will see you immediately."

Georgia Rushe weighed about a hundred and fourteen. She wasn't as young as I'd thought when I had sized up the shadow on the door—somewhere around thirty-one or thirty-two, and she didn't carry her head on one

side. That cocking to one side of the head that we'd seen
when she stood at the corridor door must have meant
that she was listening.

Bertha Cool beamed at her and said in a voice that
dripped sweetness, "Won't you be seated, Miss Rushe?"

Miss Rushe looked at me.

She had dark, emotional eyes, full lips, high cheek
bones, a smooth olive skin, and very dark hair. The way
she looked at me you'd have thought she was about to
turn and run out of the office.

Bertha said hastily, "This is Donald Lam, my partner."

Miss Rushe said, "Oh!"

"Come in, come in," Bertha invited. "Sit down in that
chair, Miss Rushe."

She still hesitated.

I gave a deep yawn without making any attempt to
cover it, took a notebook from my pocket, said casually,
"Well, I'll go cover that matter we were talking about—
or," I added as an afterthought, turning to Miss Rushe,
"do you want me to sit in on this?"

I made my tone sound somewhat bored as though another job would be just another chore. I heard Bertha
gasp and start to say something, but Georgia Rushe
smiled at me, said, "I think I'd like to have you sit in
on it," and walked over and settled herself in the big
chair.

Bertha's face was beaming. "Yes, yes, Miss Rushe.
What is it?"

"I want some help."

"Well, that's what we're here for."

She toyed with her purse for a minute, crossed her
knees, carefully smoothed her skirt down, her eyes avoid-
ing those of Bertha.

She had nice legs.

Bertha said enticingly, "Anything we can do—"

Georgia Rushe hastily averted her eyes.

I took a notebook from my pocket and scribbled a
note to Bertha Cool: *Quit being so eager. People want*

results. No one wants to hire a big-boned woman detective who's all sticky with sweetness.

I tore the page out of my notebook and slid it across the desk to Bertha.

Georgia Rushe watched Bertha pick up the note and read it.

Bertha's face got red. She crumpled the note, slammed it in the wastebasket, glowered at me.

"Okay, Miss Rushe," I said casually, "what's *your* trouble?"

Georgia Rushe took a deep breath and said, "I don't want to be censured."

"No one is going to censure you."

"I don't want to have to listen to any moral lectures."

"You won't."

She glanced apprehensively at Bertha and said, "A woman might not be as tolerant."

Bertha smiled all over her face, said coyly, "Oh, my *dear*," then suddenly remembering my note jerked herself back into character and said abruptly, "To hell with that stuff. What's on your mind?"

"To begin with," Georgia Rushe said determinedly, "I'm a home wrecker."

"So what?" Bertha asked.

"I don't want to listen to any moral lectures when you hear what I've done."

"Got enough money to pay our bills?" Bertha asked.

"Yes, of course, otherwise I wouldn't be here."

Bertha said grimly, "Go ahead and wreck 'em all you want, dearie. What do you want us to do? Scout out good homes for you to wreck? We can do it."

Miss Rushe laughed nervously, then said after a moment, "I'm glad you're taking it that way, Mrs. Cool."

Bertha said, "Homes aren't wrecked. They wreck themselves."

Georgia Rushe said, "I've been with Mr. Crail for nearly four years now."

"Who's Mr. Crail?" Bertha asked.

"Ellery Crail, the head of the Crail Venetian Blind

Company."

"I've heard of the company. How long's he been married?"

"Eight months."

I settled back and lit a cigarette.

Georgia Rushe said, "I started working in the personnel department. At that time, Ellery was married. His wife died shortly after I came to work. It left him rather dazed. I don't know how much he loved her, but he certainly missed her when she was gone. He's a man who would love a home, a great big, loyal, stouthearted man who is so fair and square himself that he just can't imagine anyone being otherwise."

She hesitated for a moment, then sighed deeply, and went on: "After a while he began to get over the first numbing shock of the grief, and—well, I saw a little something of him."

"You mean he took you out?" Bertha asked.

"We went out to dinner once or twice, yes."

"Theater?"

"Yes."

"Call at your apartment?"

"No."

"You at his?"

"No. He isn't that sort."

"When did his present wife meet him?"

Georgia Rushe said, "I was run down from overwork. We'd had a lot of problems to deal with. Mr. Crail thought I should take a long vacation and suggested I leave for a month. When I came back he was married."

"Slipped a fast one over on you?"

Georgia Rushe's eyes blazed. "He was the victim of a shrewd, scheming, designing, hypocritical, sniveling, mealymouthed individual, if you can flatter a negative personality like that by calling her an individual."

"She gave him the rush act?" Bertha asked.

"Very much so."

"How did it happen?"

"It all began one night when Mr. Crail was driving his

automobile back from work. He doesn't see too well at night, and it had been raining and the streets were slippery. Even so, I don't think it was entirely his fault, although he tries to make out that it was. There was a coupé immediately ahead of him, and a signal changed and the coupé came to a sudden stop. The brake light wasn't working. Of course, Irma swore that she put out her hand to signal a stop, but she'd swear to anything that would feather her own nest."

"Irma is the girl?"

"Yes."

"What happened?"

"Mr. Crail bumped the back of her car—not particularly hard so far as the actual damage to the automobile was concerned. Fifty dollars would have covered both cars."

"Personal injuries?" Bertha asked.

"Some sort of a spinal injury. Ellery jumped out of his car and ran up to the car ahead. He started apologizing as though it had been all his fault, just as soon as he saw the car was operated by a woman. And Irma Begley looked up at Ellery's big strong face, and into his sympathetic eyes and determined she was going to marry him —and she didn't lose any time."

"The sympathy racket?" Bertha asked.

"Apparently, a little bit of everything. Ellery's wife had died and he was lonely. He'd grown to depend on me a lot more than he realized, and then I'd gone away. Afterward, I found in the files a wire he had sent, asking me if I could possibly cut my vacation short and return. For some reason the wire was never delivered. If it had been, it might have changed my whole life. As it was, he thought I simply hadn't answered."

I looked at my watch.

Miss Rushe hurried on. "Well, Irma Begley was very nice about it, but she thought that Mr. Crail would prefer to have the car repaired himself so that he'd be certain he wasn't being victimized, and Ellery thought that was very very fair and considerate, so naturally with true magnanimity he had the whole damn car overhauled. Everything a mechanic could find wrong with it was fixed. Then he returned it to Irma, and by that time, Irma was beginning to have headaches so she went to see a doctor, and the doctor took X-rays, and then it appeared that her spine had been injured. And she was *so* brave and *so* sweet and *so* self-effacing about the whole business!

"Well, of course, Irma let Ellery see that she wasn't in any position to support herself without work, and so Ellery insisted on footing bills, and—of course no one knows *just* how it happened, but I returned from a month's vacation to find my boss on his honeymoon!"

"How long ago?"

"Six months."

"What happened then?"

"Well, at first the boss seemed sort of dazed with the suddenness of it all. He was particularly embarrassed when he was with me. He felt that he owed me some sort of an explanation as to how it happened and yet he was too much of a gentleman to say even a word about it."

"What did you do?" Bertha asked.

"I was too angry and hurt to make things easy for him. I told him I was going to quit as soon as he could get someone else to take my place. Well, he couldn't get anyone to take my place, and then he asked me to *please* stay with him and—and, well, I did."

"When did you determine you were going to be a home wrecker?"

"To tell you the truth, Mrs. Cool, I don't know. At first I was completely crushed. I felt that the bottom had dropped out of everything. I didn't realize how much I was in love with Ellery until after—well, after things seemed to be irrevocably broken."

"I know," Bertha said. "I'm trying to find out the facts."

"Well, after all, Mrs. Cool, I don't know as it's important, because that doesn't enter into it except incidentally. I wanted to get that over with first because I didn't want you to find out about it afterward and start getting upstage on me."

"But you've made up your mind you're going after Mr. Crail?"

"I've made up my mind that I'm not going to put any obstacle in the way of his going after me."

"And he's showing some indications?"

"He's dazed and he's hurt. He's wandering around in a fog."

"And beginning to gravitate toward you for guidance?"

Georgia Rushe met Bertha Cool's eyes. "Let's be frank about it, Mrs. Cool. I think he's realized that he's made a terrific mistake—and I think he realized it very shortly after I came back."

"But he's too loyal to do anything about it?"

"Yes."

"Yet you think he may do something?"

"He may."

"And if he does, you're going to make it easy for him?"

Georgia Rushe said determinedly, "That little scheming trollop stole him from me. She deliberately played her cards so she had him all tied up before I got back. I'm going to steal him back."

Bertha said, "All right, we have the background. Go ahead and tell us what's on your mind."

"Do you know anything about the Stanberry Building?"

Bertha shook her head, then said, "Wait a minute. It's out on Seventh Street, isn't it?"

Georgia Rushe nodded. "A four-story building—stores on the lower floor, offices on the second floor, the Rimley Rendezvous on the third floor and apartments for Mr. Rimley and some of his executives on the fourth floor."

"What about the Stanberry Building?"

"She wants Ellery to buy it for her."

"Why the Stanberry Building?" I asked.

"I don't know, but I think it has something to do with the night club."

"What is there about the night club that makes the

building such a marvelous investment?"

"I don't know. Pittman Rimley has four or five places scattered around town. I think he's the only one who's been able to make a success out of combining a lunch trade, swinging into an afternoon pickup business, and then operating as a night club. He rotates his floor shows and seems to do a very good business."

"What do you mean a pickup business?" Bertha asked.

"Afternoons," she said. "Women gravitate into these Rendezvous joints for a cocktail and there's dance music and pickups."

"Crail has money?" I asked.

She said evasively, "I think the Venetian blind business has been very profitable."

"He has money?"

"Yes—quite a bit."

"And just what do you want us to do?"

She said, "I want you to find out what's back of it all. She's rotten to the core, and I want you to find out what's going on."

Bertha Cool said, "All that's going to cost you money."

"How much?"

"Two hundred dollars for a starter."

Georgia Rushe was coldly businesslike. "To just what does that two hundred dollars entitle me, Mrs. Cool?"

Bertha hesitated.

I said, "It entitles you to ten days' work."

"Less expenses," Bertha snapped, hastily.

"What can you find out in that time?" Georgia Rushe asked.

Bertha said crisply, "We're detectives, not clairvoyants. How the hell should I know?"

That seemed to be the right answer. Georgia Rushe opened her purse. "No one must know that I'm back of this," she said.

Bertha Cool nodded. Her greedy little eyes fastened on the purse.

Georgia Rushe took out a checkbook.

Bertha fairly shoved the fountain pen into her hand.

Chapter Two

LEG WORK

BERTHA HELPED HERSELF TO A CIGARETTE, said to me, "Well, that's the way it goes."

"It's okay."

"Just a little piddling case for a woman who's eating her heart out, and has an exaggerated idea of what a detective agency can do."

"It's okay, Bertha."

"When you went away," Bertha said, "you'd got us into the big-time stuff. Damned if I know how you did it. You could take even the most insignificant little case, and before you got done it developed into big business and big money. Then after you left, I could take what seemed to be the biggest case and it would peter out into little business and little money. I did all right for a while. Two or three cases went just as though you'd been here. And then the bottom dropped out and it's been a whole procession of little stuff like this."

"Don't bother about it. I'll take over on this."

"What are you going to do?"

"Consult the Bureau of Vital Statistics, get whatever dope is available on the present Mrs. Crail, find out where she lived before she was married, make an investigation there, find out where she lived before that, try to find out why her sudden interest in the Stanberry Building."

"That's a lot of leg work," Bertha said.

"That's all marching is," I said, and walked out.

Elsie Brand looked up from her typewriter. "Out for the day," I told her, "working on a case. I'll telephone in later on in the afternoon and see if there's anything new."

Elsie hesitated a minute as though trying to say something, then, after a moment, her face turned red. What-

ever it was she was going to say, she didn't get it out.
She turned swiftly in her chair and hid her embarrass-
ment over the rattling keyboard of her typewriter.

I picked up the agency car from the parking-station
where we'd always kept it. The last eighteen months
seemed like a dream. I was picking up the threads of
life where I'd dropped them.

The statistical information showed that Ellery Crail
was thirty-eight, Irma Begley twenty-seven; that Crail
had been married once before and was a widower; that
Irma Begley had not been married. She had lived at
1891 Latonia Boulevard.

I drove out to the address on Latonia. It was a modest,
four-story, brick apartment house with a stucco front,
and an ornate doorway. It bore the sign, *Maplegrove
Apartments*, and a notice stating there was no vacancy.
I rang the bell marked manager and had to wait for
nearly five minutes.

The manager turned out to be a fleshy woman somewhere around forty, with shrewd little black eyes, full
thick lips, and a perfect complexion. At the start, she
was as belligerent, and looked as formidable, as a big
tank. Then I smiled at her and, after a moment, she
smiled back at me and became kittenish.

"I'm *so* sorry. There isn't a vacancy in the place,
and—"

"I wanted a little information about a woman who
used to live here."

"What about her?"

"A Miss— Miss—" I made a great show of having forgotten the name and fished a notebook from my pocket,
ran my finger down the page and said, "A Miss Latham
. . . No, wait a minute. That isn't the one." I ran my
finger down a few more lines and said, "Begley, Irma
Begley."

"She used to live here. She got married."

"Do you know whom she married?"

"No, I don't. I think it was a pretty good match. She
was rather uncommunicative."

"You were manager at the time?"

"That's right."

"Know anything about her—who her folks were? Where she came from, or anything?"

"No. She didn't even leave a forwarding address when she left. I found out afterward she'd gone down to the post office and taken care of that herself."

"Isn't that rather unusual?"

"Yes. They usually leave a forwarding address in case anything happens to come here."

I said, "Well, how about when she rented the apartment in the first place, she must have given some references?"

"Oh, yes."

"Suppose we could look them up?"

"Just what was your name?" she asked.

I smiled at her and said, "You won't believe me."

"Why not?"

"It's Smith."

"I don't."

"People seldom do."

"Won't you come in, Mr. Smith?"

"Thanks."

The manager's apartment was on the ground floor and was overfurnished and smelled of sandalwood. A Chinese incense burner on a table in the center of the room was sending out wisps of white smoke. There were too many pictures on the wall, too many chairs, too many tables, and too many nicknacks.

"Won't you sit down, Mr. Smith?"

"Thanks." I offered her a cigarette. She took one and I held a match.

"Just why did you want to know?"

I looked blank.

"I mean what's the object in getting the information?"

I said, "Shucks, I don't know. They never tell me. Just hand me a list of names, tell me to find out certain things. It may be she's applied for an insurance policy, or it might be an old bill, or perhaps she's inherited money and they're trying to locate her to close up an estate."

"She was a very nice girl," the manager said.

I blew out cigarette smoke and said, "Uh huh."

"Very quiet as I remember her, and kept very much to herself. No wild parties."

"That's nice."

"She wasn't the type that would have any unpaid bills."

"Then it can't be an unpaid bill," I said.

"But *you* don't know what it is?"

"That's right. Someone wants to know, that's all. That's my business, investigating. I get a dollar a name and furnish my own expenses."

She said, "I have a few people *I'd* like to know about."

"Give me their names. I'd have to turn them in through the office. I don't know just how the office handles it. There's some charge for a retainer. You have to guarantee so much business in the course of a month or a year or whatever it is, and, of course, they charge you more than a dollar. A dollar is my cut."

She said, "Well, when you put it that way, it's not worth much to me to find them, because you can't get blood out of a turnip. Let me see what I can find."

She opened a drawer in a flat-topped desk, pulled out some cards and started riffling through a classification marked *Ba-Be.*

After a moment, she found the card she wanted, pulled it out, said, "That's right, Irma Begley. She lived at 392 South Fremington Street before she came here."

"Give any references?" I asked.

"Two. Benjamin C. Cosgate and Frank L. Glimson."

"Any address?"

The manager said, "It's a downtown business address —and that's all the information we have about her except that she paid her rent promptly, and was listed as a good tenant."

"All right, that's all I need," I said. "Thanks a lot."

The manager said, "If you can get enough of them in

a day, you should be able to make money at that."

I said, "You have to keep jumping around."

"Yes, I hadn't thought of that. Paying your own expenses makes a difference. How much information do you have to get?"

"Oh, enough to let them know whatever it is they want to find out. Sometimes it's easy. Sometimes it's quite a job. Most of the time you can count on an average of forty-five minutes to a name. Well, I've got a couple of more names in the neighborhood—try to group them all together."

"I hope you find what you want, Mr. Smith," she said.

"Thank you," I told her.

A telephone book in a near-by drugstore showed me that Benjamin C. Cosgate was a lawyer, Frank Glimson was a lawyer, and there was a firm of Cosgate & Glimson.

I started to call them, then thought better of it and postponed it until after I'd driven once more to the courthouse.

This time I looked at the Register of Actions, Plaintiff, and read through so many names that I all but passed up the one I wanted, but there it was: *Irma Begley versus Philip E. Cullingdon.* I made a note of the number of the case, told the deputy clerk I was a lawyer looking up some of the old records, and asked for files on the case.

There was a neat little complaint, a demurrer, an amended complaint, a demurrer to an amended complaint, and a notice of dismissal. Attorneys for the plaintiff were Cosgate & Glimson.

I skimmed through the complaint. It stated that on the fifth day of April, 1942, while the plaintiff had been driving and operating a motor vehicle in a careful and law-abiding manner, the defendant, without due or any regard for the safety of other vehicles or the occupants thereof, had so carelessly, negligently, and unlawfully driven and operated his automobile over, along, and upon a certain public highway known as Wilshire Boulevard, that he had caused his said automobile to collide with the automobile driven by the plaintiff; that as a result of said collision, plaintiff had sustained a permanent injury of the spine which had necessitated the payment of doctor bills in the amount of two hundred and fifty dollars, nursing and medicine in the amount of eighty-five dollars and twenty cents, X-rays in an amount of seventy-five dollars, and specialist fees in an amount of five hundred dollars; that plaintiff was permanently injured, and that the careless driving of the defendant's automobile as aforesaid was the sole and proximate cause of said injury. Wherefore, Plaintiff prayed judgment in an amount of fifty thousand dollars and for her costs of suit incurred herein.

The suit had been filed on the thirty-first day of March, 1943.

I made a few notes from the papers, getting the names and addresses of the defendant's lawyers, and looked in the telephone book for Philip E. Cullingdon. I found him listed as a contractor and made a note of his residence. Then I went down the hall to a telephone booth, called the office, found Bertha Cool was out, told Elsie Brand I was going to drop around for a cocktail at the Rimley Rendezvous; that if anything important turned up, Bertha could reach me there. Elsie asked me how I was doing on the case, and I told her I was making a little progress—nothing to write home about, but getting a few leads, and hung up.

Chapter Three

THE RIMLEY RENDEZVOUS

AT ONE TIME the Rendezvous idea had swept the country like a plague. Night clubs built up a fine afternoon trade, catering to women between thirty and forty who wanted romance. Some of these women were grass widows on the make. Some of them were married women who kidded their husbands and perhaps themselves, pretending they'd been shopping and had "just dropped in" for a drink.

It was a nice racket for the night clubs, who found themselves suddenly catering to a very profitable afternoon business—for a while. Then the grief began to catch up. The men who hung around didn't do the places any good. The general nature of the setup began to leak out, and the first thing these places knew, they were writing the answers in red ink.

Most of them began to put drastic regulations into effect—no unescorted women, no table hopping.

The Rimley Rendezvous kept open and, as nearly as I could tell, there were no restrictions, which was interesting.

Because the Stanberry Building was on the edge of a congested business district, it was hard to find a parking place. There was a parking-lot in the middle of the next block, and I was heading for it when I got a break. A taxi moved out from in front of the entrance to the building and I spotted a space between the painted strip of curb which marked the loading-zone and taxi stand and a big Cadillac parked just behind. There was barely room to squeeze in. I didn't intend to stay long and acted on the assumption the big Cad might belong to one of the big shots. I squeezed the agency car up pretty close. After I got out, I saw it was even closer than I'd thought, but I left it there anyway.

The elevator shot me up to the Rimley Rendezvous—a faint hint of heady perfume, deep carpets, subdued lights, dreamy music, swift-moving, solicitous waiters—an atmosphere of clandestine class, coupled with security and stability. A swell setup.

I had a Scotch and soda. It was served in an amber glass so I couldn't see how pale the drink was. Even if Pittman Rimley was paying twenty dollars a bottle for his Scotch, he could still make money at the prices he was charging and the amount of liquor he was putting in the drinks.

The place had a marvelous orchestra, quite a few women, and a sprinkling of men—the fat-faced executive type who had stayed over from the merchant's lunch, the poker-faced guys with long sideburns who kept their stomachs lean and hard, and tried to look like movie actors. It never had been much of a spot for the younger type. That class couldn't stand the tariff.

A voice came drifting over my shoulder. The accents were those of routine seduction, "Cigars—cigarettes?"

I turned around and got an eyeful. She was about twenty-three with a skirt that stopped two or three inches before it reached her knees, a fancy white apron, a blouse with wide, flaring collar and a low V in front. The conventional tray suspended from the shoulder harness held an assortment of cigars, cigarettes, and bonbons.

I paid two-bits of Georgia Rushe's expense money for a package of cigarettes, ostensibly on the theory that I might open up a contact, actually because I was enjoying the scenery.

She had whimsical light gray eyes that smiled a sophisticated "thank you," and seemed to have a somewhat detached, philosophical consideration for men who liked to look at legs.

She didn't move away, but waited to strike a match for me.

"Thanks," I said.

"It's a pleasure."

I liked her voice, but that was all I heard of it. She gave me another smile and moved away.

I looked the place over and wondered if by any chance Mrs. Ellery Crail might be among those present. I didn't see any women who would have fitted the description and the part. Anemic, female droops didn't go in for afternoon romance. It took women with a restless sex consciousness to patronize a place like that.

There wasn't any use losing any sleep over it. I had a routine chore of detective work at ten bucks per day, and there was no occasion to use a lot of finesse. I walked out to the telephone booth and called the agency.

Bertha was out. I gave careful instructions to Elsie Brand. "I'm at the Rimley Rendezvous. I want to get a line on a woman here. Take a look at your watch. Wait exactly seven minutes, then call the Rendezvous and ask if Mrs. Ellery Crail is here. Say that you'd like to have her come to the telephone, to page her if they don't know her, that it's important. Wait until they go to get her and then hang up."

"Anything else?"

"Nope. That's all."

"Any messages you want to leave for Bertha?"

"Tell her I'm down here."

"Okay, Donald. Good to hear your voice."

"Good to hear yours. Good-by."

I went back to my table. The waiter was hovering around as though I hadn't been drinking my liquor fast enough. So I finished it up and ordered another.

The drink came just about at the expiration of the seven minutes.

I started looking around. The head waiter summoned one of the underlings, said something to him and the man nodded, moved very unobtrusively over to a table where a woman and a man were sitting. He said something to the woman and she got up and excused herself.

At first I couldn't believe it. Then I saw from the way she walked as she headed toward the telephone that she must be the one I wanted. There was a little one-sided hitch to the walk. It wasn't a limp, it was simply a vague stiffness as the back got in just one position.

But she wasn't anything like Georgia Rushe had described her. She wasn't any anemic little milksop. She was all woman, and she knew it. The cardigan suit was smooth over well-shaped hips; her chin was tilted at a saucy angle, and there was pert independence in the way she carried her head. When she walked, men turned to look at her and, in that environment, that alone spoke volumes.

While she was out at the telephone I looked at the man who was with her. He was a tall drink of water with all the robust sex magnetism of a marble slab. He looked like a bank cashier with a passion for exact figures—on paper. You couldn't picture him as getting enthusiastic over any others. You felt certain his fingers knew their way around on the keyboard of an adding machine. He was somewhere around fifty with the expression amateur theatrical players like to assume when they're taking the part of an English butler.

A couple of minutes later, Mrs. Crail returned to the table. The man who was with her arose and seated her with punctilious, unsmiling formality. Then he settled back in his seat and they talked in low tones.

For all of the expression on their faces, they might have been discussing the national debt.

I left the table once more, sauntered to the telephone booth, and again called the office. Elsie Brand told me Bertha Cool was in now, and I told her to put Bertha on the line.

"Hello," Bertha said. "Where the hell are you, lover?"

"Down at the Rimley Rendezvous."

"Are you still there?"

"Yes."

"That's a hell of a way to work on a case," she said angrily, "sitting at a table guzzling drinks on the expense account and—"

"Shut up," I interrupted, "and get this straight. Mrs. Ellery Crail is here with a man. I don't think they're going to stay long. I'd like to know who the man is. Suppose you stick around the outside, pick them up when they come out and tail them."

"You've got the agency car."

"You have your personal car, haven't you?"

"Well . . . Yes."

I said, "Mrs. Crail is about twenty-eight. She weighs a hundred and twelve pounds. She's five foot four and a half inches tall, is dressed in a black dressy suit, a large black straw hat with a red doodad on it, red reptile shoes, and a red bag.

"The man who's with her is fifty-two, five feet ten, a hundred and seventy-one to a hundred and seventy-five, double-breasted bluish gray suit with a white pin stripe, long nose, long jaw, an expressionless map, dark blue necktie with a red pattern in big S curves, edged with white, sandy complexion, eyes either gray or light blue, I can't tell which at this distance.

"You can pick up the woman by watching her walk. She swings her legs from the hips. But when she swings her right leg, the left side of her back has just a slight hitch. You'll have to watch sharp to notice it, but if you watch sharp, you *will* notice it."

Bertha, somewhat mollified, said, "Well, that's all right, if you've got them spotted. I'm glad you've accomplished something. I'll come right down. You don't think I'd better go inside the club and wait?"

"I wouldn't. I'd wait on the outside. It might be a little too noticeable if you got up and went out at the same time they did. They may be just a little suspicious after that telephone call that didn't materialize."

"All right, lover, I'll take care of it."

I went back and sat down at the table. The waiter, I noticed, was watching me rather closely.

"Cigars—cigarettes?"

The voice with the smile was right over my shoulder. I turned and looked at the legs. "Hello," I said. "I just bought a pack of cigarettes. Remember? I don't use them up that fast."

She leaned slightly forward, said in a low voice, "Buy another one. You seem to enjoy the scenery, and I want to talk with you."

I started to make a wisecrack then caught the expression in her eyes and reached in my pocket for another quarter. "It's a fair exchange," I said.

She placed a package of cigarettes on the table, leaned forward to take my quarter and said, *"Get out!"*

I raised my eyebrows at her.

She smiled tolerantly as though I'd made some verbal pass, and tore off the corner of the cigarette package for me. She took out one and extended it to me. "You're Donald Lam, aren't you?" she asked, striking a match.

This time I didn't need to raise my eyebrows. They popped up by themselves. "How," I asked, "do *you* know?"

"Don't be silly. Use your head. You've got one."

She leaned forward and applied the match to the end of the cigarette. "Leaving?"

"No."

She said, "Then for heaven's sake, circulate! Pick up some of these women who are looking you over with purring approval. The way it is now, you stand out like a sore thumb."

That was an idea. I realized suddenly that unattached men didn't drop into the Rendezvous simply to sip a highball. But I was still worried about how the cigarette girl had learned my name. I'd been in the Southwest Pacific for some eighteen months now. And before that I didn't think I was particularly well known as a figure about town.

The dance orchestra started making noise. I picked a young, vivacious-looking brunette a couple of tables over. She seemed just a little *too* demure as I walked over.

"Dance?" I asked.

She looked up at me with a well-simulated expression of haughty surprise. "Why—aren't you being just a little abrupt?"

I met her eyes and said, "Yes."

That brought a laugh. "I like abrupt men," she said, and arose to extend her arms to me.

We danced half around the floor without saying anything. Then she said, "Somehow you aren't the type I had pictured."

"What do you mean by that?"

"The way you sat over there frowning into your drink —you looked melancholy and belligerent."

"Perhaps it was belligerency."

"No. I was wondering about you. Oh, I suppose I've given myself away that I was watching you."

"Any harm in watching me?"

"One isn't supposed to admit it."

I didn't say anything and we danced some more. Then she laughed and said, "I was right all the time. You are belligerent and melancholy."

I said, "Let's talk about you for a while. Who are the two women with you?"

"Friends."

"You surprise me."

She said, "The three of us go around together quite a lot. We have something in common."

"Married?"

"Well. . . . No, not that."

"Divorced?"

"Yes."

We danced some more. She said, "You don't come here very often, do you?"

"No."

"I haven't seen you. I wondered—something about you. You don't look like the sort of man who does come here. You're hard and—well, there's nothing aimless or smirking about you."

"What about the men who come here?" I asked.

"Most of them are no good. Occasionally you see someone who is—interesting. It's once in a blue moon. There, I'm giving myself away again."

"You like to dance, and occasionally you find a partner here, is that right?"

"That's about it."

The music stopped. I took her back to her table. She said coyly, "If I knew your name, I'd present you to my friends."

"I never tell my name."

"Why?"

"I'm not the sort you'd like to present to your friends."

"Why?"

I said, "I'm married. I have three children who are starving. I can't support my wife because I spend my afternoons in places like this. Time and again I've made up my mind to cut it out. But I just can't do it. I'll be walking along the street and see a beautiful face and figure like yours headed into one of these joints, and immediately I go plunging in after it, spending my last cent just for the pleasure of talking with you, holding you in my arms while I dance around a crowded floor."

We were at the table now. She laughed and said, "Girls, I think his name is John Smith. He has the most *delightful* line."

Two new feminine faces looked up at me with amused interest.

The head waiter stood close to me. "I beg your pardon, sir."

"What rule have I violated now?" I asked.

"Nothing, sir. But the manager asked me to present his compliments and ask you to join him for a few moments. It's quite important."

"Well, I like *that!*" the girl with whom I had been dancing said.

The waiter remained silently insistent at my elbow.

I smiled at the three young women, said, "After all, I can be back, you know," and then followed my guide out through the main doorway, through a curtained doorway into an anteroom, then through a door marked *Private* which the head waiter opened without knocking.

He said, "Mr. Lam for you, sir," and retired, pulling the massive door closed behind him.

The man who was seated behind the big polished walnut desk looked up from some papers and his eyes hit mine; hard, dark, restless eyes that threw out the magnetic fire of a dynamic personality.

A smile softened the heavy mouth. The man pushed back the swivel chair and came around the desk.

He wasn't particularly tall and he wasn't fat, but he was thick all the way through, thick-chested, thick-necked, and a body that went straight up and down, with few curves. A tailor had done a marvelous job on him, and there was a well-groomed appearance about his hair that indicated a barber had spent quite a bit of time in painstaking toil. Every hair was smoothly tailored into place.

"How are you, Mr. Lam? My name is Rimley. I own the place."

I shook hands.

He sized me up thoughtfully, said, "Sit down. Care for a cigar?"

"No thanks. I smoke cigarettes."

He opened a humidor on his desk. "I think you'll find your favorite brand here. I—"

"No thanks, I have a package in my pocket I want to get smoked up."

I fumbled in my pocket. It occurred to me that it might be very bad business, at the moment, to let him know about that second pack of cigarettes.

"Well, do sit down and make yourself comfortable. Care for a drink?"

"I've just had two of your Scotch and sodas."

He laughed and said, "I mean a *real* drink."

"Scotch and soda," I said.

He picked up a desk telephone, flipped over a switch, and said, "Two Scotch and sodas, my private brand."

He clicked the switch off and said, "Just back from the South Pacific, I understand."

"May I ask how you know?"

He made arches out of his eyebrows, "Why not?"

There wasn't any answer, so I went back to first principles. "I've been away for quite a while. While you were in business when I left, I don't think I'd ever been out here. It just happened I hadn't ever dropped in."

"That is why your present visit interests me."

"But how did it happen you knew who I was?"

He said, "Come, come, Mr. Lam. We're realists, both of us."

"Suppose we are?"

"Put yourself in my position. In order to run a place like this, one has to be on the black side of the ledger. One has to make money."

"Naturally."

"In order to make money, one has to put himself in the position of his customers. What do they come here for? What do they want? What do they seek? What do they get? What do they pay for? Obviously, Mr. Lam, if you'd put yourself in *my* place, and remember I am trying to think in terms of customers' wants, you will readily understand that the unannounced visit of a private detective is—well, it's something to be reported to me."

"Yes, I can see that. Do you know *all* the private detectives?"

"Certainly not. But I know the ones who are smart enough to be dangerous."

"How do you segregate?"

"I don't. They segregate themselves."

"I'm afraid I don't follow you."

"Being a private detective is like following any other profession. The incompetent ones have a tendency to weed themselves out. The ones who can just get by remain unknown, with only a nominal business. The ones who have what it takes begin to attract attention. They begin to get more and more business. People begin to talk about them. I know all of those."

"You flatter me."

"Don't be so damn modest. Before you enlisted in the Navy, you'd made quite a name for yourself, a little guy with guts—guts and brains; a daring operator who played a no-limit game and always brought his clients out on top. I watched your career with a great deal of interest. I thought I might need you myself, sometime.

"And then, of course, there's your partner, Bertha Cool. Rather an outstanding figure."

"You've known her for some time?"

"Frankly, I never bothered with her until you teamed up with her and organized that partnership. Bertha was on my list, of course—one of the few agencies that would take domestic-relations cases. But nothing that needed to occupy my personal attention. She handled routine stuff in a routine way. Then you came along and you began handling routine stuff in a very unconventional manner. The cases you handled ceased to be routine."

"You know a lot about me," I said.

He nodded calmly, matter-of-factly, as one agreeing with an obvious fact. "I know a hell of a lot about you."

"And why am I honored this afternoon?"

Knuckles tapped on the door.

"Come in," Rimley called.

I noticed a slight movement of the right side of his body, heard a muffled click. The door opened and a waiter came in bearing a tray with glasses, a bottle of Johnny Walker Black Label, a container filled with ice cubes, and a big quart bottle of siphon water.

The waiter put the tray down on the corner of the desk, walked out without a word. Rimley poured two big slugs of whisky into the glasses, dropped in ice cubes, squirted in soda, handed me a glass.

"Regards," he said.

"Regards," I replied.

We took a sip from the glasses. Rimley swung around in the chair, smiled, and said, "I hope I don't have to dot the i's and cross the t's."

"You mean that you don't want me here?"

"Definitely."

"Is there," I asked, "anything you can do about it?"

His eyes were hard now, but his lips were still smiling. "Quite a bit," he said.

"I'm interested. Barring the minor subterfuges of telling me the tables are all engaged, or instructing the waiters not to wait on me, I don't see anything very subtle or very effective that you could do."

He smiled and said, "Have you ever noticed, Lam, that the persons who talk about what they're going to do very seldom do what they say they're going to do?"

I nodded.

"I never talk about what I'm going to do. I do it. And, above all, I wouldn't be so foolish as to tell *you* what I was going to do to keep you from being a regular visitor. Working on some particular case?"

I smiled and said, "Just dropped in because I wanted a little social life."

"Obviously," Rimley said smiling, "you can appreciate the reactions of my customers if someone should point you out and say, 'That's Donald Lam of the firm of Cool & Lam, private detectives. They're one of the firms that handle divorce cases.' I rather fancy there'd be lots of diners who would very suddenly remember they had engagements elsewhere."

I said, "I hadn't exactly thought of that particular angle."

"Suppose you think of it now, then."

We sipped our drinks.

"I'm thinking of it," I said.

I wondered if Mrs. Crail and her escort had left the place yet, and if Bertha Cool was on the job. I also wondered if Pittman Rimley's aversion to private detectives might not be due, at least in part, to the fact that he may have had some idea that a sale of the building in which his club was located was in process of negotiation—and did his lease have a clause that changed its terms in the event the premises were sold?

Rimley said, "Well, don't let it get you down, Lam. How about freshening up your drink?"

He reached across for my glass with his left hand, held the bottle of Scotch over the glass, gurgled in amber liquid, and squirted in siphon water.

I don't know just how it happened that my eyes dropped down for a casual glance at the very expensive wrist chronometer with its sweep second hand circling the dial, but they did. It was a big watch and only a big man could have worn it, but it was a watch that could keep time to a split fraction of a second.

The watch said four-thirty.

I did mental arithmetic. It couldn't have been that late. I wanted to look at my own watch, but somehow it didn't seem to be just the thing to do.

Rimley freshened up his own drink, smiled at me across the brim of the glass. "After all," he said, "just so we understand each other."

"Certainly," I told him. "That's all that's necessary."

I looked around the office very casually.

There was a clock on top of a filing-case, one of those nautical affairs mounted inside the spokes of a bronze wheel.

I waited until Rimley was looking at something else then flashed my eyes back for a quick glance at the face of the clock.

The time was four thirty-two.

I said, "You must have your problems running a place of this kind."

"It isn't all gravy," he admitted.

"I suppose you get to know your customers pretty well?"

"The regular ones, yes."

"Have trouble getting liquor?"

"Some."

"I've got a client who wants to bring suit against some people for an automobile accident. Know any good lawyers?"

"Is that the case that you're working on now?"

I simply smiled.

"Pardon me," he said.

"Know any good automobile accident lawyers?" I asked.

"No."

"Guess there are some pretty good ones around."

"There should be."

I said, "Well, it's nice liquor and I've enjoyed my visit. I suppose you'd prefer I didn't go back to my table."

"Go right ahead, Lam. Make yourself at home. Enjoy yourself. Relax. Have a good time. And when you leave, don't bother about the check. Just get up and walk out. There won't be any check. But *don't—come—back!*"

He'd been holding me with liquor and talk. Now both the liquor and the talk had dried up. It was quite all right for me to go back to the Rendezvous—now. Why had he been so anxious to get me out of the place a few minutes before and was so willing to let me return now? Could it be because Mrs. Ellery Crail and her escort had left?

I tossed off the last of the drink, got up, and extended my hand. "Nice meeting you," I said.

"Thank you. Make yourself at home, Lam. Have a good time, and I wish you every success with whatever case you happen to be working on. Just remember to work on it some place other than here."

He followed me to the door and bowed me out.

I went back to the main dining-room.

I knew I didn't have to look. I did it just to make sure.

The table where Mrs. Ellery Crail had sat with the unsmiling individual in the double-breasted gray suit was vacant.

I looked at my watch.

The time was three forty-five.

I didn't see my cigarette girl, so I asked a waiter casually, "Cigarette girl here?"

"Yes, sir, just a moment."

A girl came toward me, legs, apron, tray, but it wasn't the same one.

I bought a package of cigarettes. "Where's the other girl?"

"Billy? Oh, she went home an hour early today. I'm filling in for her."

My girl friends over at the other table kept looking in my direction. I went over there. I didn't dance but just chatted for a minute. I was, I told them, being arrested for nonsupport of my wife and seven children. I was going to have to arrange bail, and could they do something to keep me out of jail?

I saw they were puzzled, and interested. And the waiter came along again. Mr. Rimley's compliments and would my friends care to join me in a drink on the house, some champagne, perhaps, or some of that Black Label Johnny Walker?

The young women stared as though they were seeing and hearing things. "My God," one of them said, "he must be the Duke of Windsor!"

They all laughed.

I smiled at the waiter. "My thanks to Mr. Rimley," I said. "Tell him that I enjoyed his hospitality, but I never drink more than I can hold comfortably. However, my friends will probably accept a drink on the house. I'm leaving."

"Yes, sir. There's no check, sir. Mr. Rimley's taken care of that."

"So I understand. But I suppose a tip would be in order?"

He seemed positively embarrassed. "If you don't mind, sir, I'd rather not."

I nodded, turned and bowed to the three most startled women in the city. "A business appointment," I assured them gravely, and walked out of the main dining-room.

I recovered my hat from the hat-check girl and she was perfectly willing to accept the two-bits I handed to her.

I took the elevator to the ground floor, tried to be nonchalant as I walked out and headed for the agency car. I'd misjudged the owner of the big Cad. Not only had he gone out before I did, but he'd calmly shoved his car into low gear and pushed the agency car forward so that it was right in front of the entrance of the building. A cab had moved into the place where the Cad had been parked.

A cab driver walked over to me. He had a broken nose and a cauliflower ear. "Your car?"

"Yes."

"Get it the hell out of here."

"Someone shoved it out here. I didn't leave it here."

He spat insultingly. "I've heard that one so many times it put this tin ear on me. I had to let a passenger out of my car way out from the curb. It cost me a dollar tip."

He held out his hand.

I regarded the outstretched hand gravely. "You mean you lost a dollar?"

"Yeah."

I reached for the door of the agency car. "I'm sorry, Buddy. I'm going to make it up to you."

"That's the general idea."

I said, "I'm from the income tax department. Take it off your return and tell the department I said it was okay." I started the motor.

He lunged toward me, met my eyes, hesitated.

I slammed the car door shut and drove off.

It was four twenty-three when I got to the office.

Chapter Four

TRAFFIC JAM

BERTHA CAME IN just before five. Her cheeks were flushed, her eyes glittering. She jerked the door open, strode into the office, took one look at me, and said all in one breath, "Donald, why the hell don't you go in the private office and read the newspaper?"

"I've seen the newspaper."

"Well, sit in there and twiddle your thumbs then. Don't sit out here. It takes Elsie's mind off her business."

"She's been typing right along," I said. "Anyhow, it's quitting time."

"Well," Bertha snapped, "it takes her mind off her business just the same. I'll bet she's been making mistakes."

She strode over to the typewriter, looked at the last two pages Elsie had done, and pointed an accusing finger. "There you are," she said. "An erasure, another erasure. Here's a third one."

"What of it?" I said. "Rubber companies pay dividends out of selling typewriter erasers. They know that stenographers are going to make mistakes once in a while. Three mistakes on four pages isn't too much."

"Humph! That's what *you* think. Look at these."

She ran through several other pages. There wasn't so much as the evidence of an erasure on them.

I looked at Elsie. Her cheeks were flaming red.

"A fine detective you are," Bertha grunted. "Come in."

I started to say something but Elsie's eyes were pleading with me not to, so I followed Bertha into the private office.

"A hell of a mess," Bertha said angrily, slamming back the cover of the humidor and helping herself to a cigarette.

"What's the matter, did you miss them?"

"No, I picked them up all right. She's Mrs. Ellery Crail and she's driving a Buick Roadmaster that's registered in her name. The man with her is Rufus Stanberry. He's the man who owns the building. He lives at 3271 Fulrose Avenue in the Fulrose Apartments. That's a swanky place with lots of liveried servants and a lot of gingerbread on the lobby entrance. He drives a big Cadillac."

I said, "It looks to me as though you've done a pretty good job, Bertha. What's the trouble?"

"Trouble!" Bertha all but screamed at me. "Of all the dirty damn messes!"

"Go ahead, unburden yourself."

Bertha controlled herself with an effort, said angrily, "God knows what it is. I guess it's a knack you have—something like an evil eye. Whenever you start in on a case, it *never* runs smooth. Something always goes sour."

I fished out one of the packages of cigarettes I had bought from the girl at the Rendezvous and shook out a cigarette.

Bertha's hand jerked toward the humidor on the desk. "Use one of these, lover, during office hours. I charge them to office expense."

I conveyed my cigarette to my lips, put the pack back in the pocket, struck a match, and said, "This is on the expense account, too."

"How come?"

"I bought it from the girl at the Rendezvous."

Bertha started to say something, then thought better of it.

I took all three packages from my pocket, placed them on the desk.

Bertha glowered. "What the hell's the idea?"

"Nothing," I said casually. "They're my brand, and she had pretty legs, that's all."

Bertha all but choked.

"Go ahead," I invited.

"Damn you," Bertha said, "I don't know whether you realize how much you irritate me."

I met her angry eyes. "Want to dissolve the partnership?"

"No!" she yelled.

"Then shut up," I said.

We locked eyes for a minute, then I gave her a chance for a diversion. "What happened when you shadowed Mrs. Crail?"

Bertha took a deep drag at the cigarette, exhaled, said, "I sat out in front of the Rendezvous. I've been there perhaps five minutes when the door opens and these two people come out. You've described them to a tee. It's like shooting fish in a rain barrel.

"They stand in front of the building for a minute, then separate. The man looks at a wrist watch, then gets in a big Cadillac. The woman goes tripping down the street. I have to make up my mind. I pick the man."

I nodded. "The man was the one I wanted."

Bertha's eyes glittered at me. "You'd jammed the agency car right up against this big Cad, and he just shoved it the hell out of there without even trying to inch his way out. Made me so damn mad I all but gave him a piece of my mind."

I didn't say anything.

"You shouldn't have left the agency car there. You'd squeezed right up against this big Cad."

I took a drag at the cigarette.

"Well," Bertha went on, "I tailed this Cad. He drove pretty fast to Garden Vista Boulevard. Then he went down the boulevard and damned if there wasn't some car tagging along behind *me!* I took a gander, and it was Mrs. Crail following this Cad."

I raised my eyebrows.

"Well, I pulled off to the right to see whether she was trying to tail me, and she slowed right down, waiting for some other car to move in. She didn't want to get close enough to the Cad so the driver could see her."

"So what did you do?" I asked.

"Well, I was in something of a spot, so I swung clean over to the right-hand traffic lane and trailed along in the blind spot of the Cad and to one side of Mrs. Crail's Buick."

"Good stuff," I said, "unless they happen to turn left."

"Well," Bertha snapped, "he turned left."

"And you lost him?"

Bertha said, "Shut up! I'm not *that* dumb!"

She puffed angrily at the cigarette for a moment, then said, "When I saw he was going to turn left, I slowed for the car that was directly behind me to go on past, then I was going to cut across to the left-hand lane of traffic. The car behind me was driven by a buck-toothed little bitch who didn't like the way I was driving. She slowed when I slowed, then suddenly pulled up abreast of me and yelled at me, something about why didn't I tell her I was going to spend my two weeks vacation in that one spot, then gave it the gun and shot on past."

"And then?" I asked.

"And then," Bertha said, "she looked to see where she was going just a little too late. Another car coming from the opposite direction was making a left-hand turn. I don't think this trollop ever saw him until half a second before the crash. Even then she might have put on the brakes and saved herself, but she was going fast and she tried to whip around the corner to the right and cut inside of him. She didn't make it."

"Anybody hurt?"

"The man wasn't, but the woman with him pulled a faint. They blocked me absolutely and completely. There was traffic behind, and this mass of wreckage right square in front of me."

"And that was when Stanberry turned left?"

"Don't be silly," Bertha said. "Traffic at that inter-section was all jammed to hell. It took a cop five minutes to get it moving. And the buck-toothed trollop flagged a taxicab that was swinging left into a parking-station and rode away just as calmly as you please, leaving her goddamned car right in *my* road."

"Without getting the names of witnesses, or seeing who—?"

Bertha said, "She gave her name and address to the driver of the other car, and she went over to Stanberry's car, got his name and address, then went around to the other cars. She even came to me. That was while traffic was jammed. It was through her that I got Stanberry's name and address."

"How come?"

"Traffic was all snarled up. The traffic coming toward town on the boulevard kept inching past and you couldn't bust into it with a chisel. Stanberry seemed very decent about it. Of course the cars behind were raising hell. The driver of the other car didn't go around any, but he was writing down license numbers. The buck-toothed biddy was turning on personality and getting names and addresses. I saw she had Stanberry's name in her book so when she came to me, instead of telling her to go to hell, I smiled sweetly at her and told her I'd be glad to, but that she'd have trouble spelling my name, and I'd better write it down for her."

"What did she do?"

"Did just what I hoped she'd do," Bertha said. "She gave me the little notebook and told me to write it down. The name directly above mine was Rufus Stanberry, 3271 Fulrose Avenue. I fumbled around with her pencil getting a good look at the names and addresses so I'd remember them, and then I wrote down a name for her."

"Your own?" I asked.

Bertha glared at me. "Don't be a fool. I thought up the damnedest Russian spelling I could think of and gave the first address that popped into my head out in Glendale, smiled sweetly at the pop-eyed little wench, and handed it back to her. Then I started signaling for the traffic behind me to get out of my way and tried backing up."

"And then what?"

"And then," she said, "I had to argue with some damn bird behind me who couldn't back up because there was somebody behind him who wouldn't back up. There was a lot of tooting horns, and I lost my temper. I tried to slam the car back and locked bumpers with some dumb egg who had come up too close behind me, and this traffic cop came along and poured acid all over everybody, and the damn horse-toothed cluck that had caused the whole business gave a sweet smile to the traffic cop, caught a taxi that was turning left into a hotel parking-stand over on Mantica, and went away and left her heap right in the street."

"What did you do?"

Bertha said, "I finally stood on my damned bumper while the other man lifted on his, and got the cars loose. By that time—"

"Did the woman get Mrs. Crail's name?"

"Sure. It was a couple of names above Stanberry's. I saw it was there. I didn't bother with the address because we have it. I was trying to find who the man was."

"Did Stanberry see Mrs. Crail's name?"

"No. I'm the only one who wrote down a name in the book. She'd done the writing on the others, also their license numbers. You can bet *I* didn't write *my* license number for her."

"So what did you do when you got free of the other car—come directly back here?"

"No. I figured she'd probably be taking Stanberry home, so I beat it out to 3271 Fulrose Avenue. I cased the joint and found it had a private switchboard, hung around there for a while, and then when they didn't show up, I decided to hell with it and came back to the office. What did *you* do?"

I said, "I got kicked out of the Rimley Rendezvous."

"Flirting with women?"

"No. The manager invited me in, bought me a drink, and told me to get out and stay out."

"He's got a crust."

"He's right," I said. "He's running a joint where married women drop in for an afternoon pickup, where a few tired businessmen hang around after the merchant's lunch to do a little casual dancing. A private detective is as welcome there as a case of smallpox on an ocean liner."

"How did he know you were a private detective?"

"That," I said, "is what gets me. He knew it. He knew my name, knew everything about me, knew all about you."

"Did he know what case you were working on?" Bertha asked.

I said, "I'm wondering whether he put two and two together; that call for Mrs. Crail, and then no one being on the telephone; the fact that Mrs. Crail and Stanberry must have left at just about the time I was being entertained in the office, and then all of a sudden Rimley wanting to terminate the interview. That *could* have been after he'd received a signal that Mrs. Crail had made her getaway. I don't think it occurred to anybody that you'd be waiting outside to pick them up, and—"

The telephone rang.

Bertha Cool scooped up the receiver. I heard Elsie Brand's voice coming through, then a click and another voice. Bertha was all suave smiles. "Yes, Miss Rushe," she said, "we're making progress. Mrs. Crail was at the Rimley Rendezvous this afternoon with Mr. Stanberry."

There was silence for a while, then Bertha said, "I'll let you talk with Donald. He's here."

She passed the phone over to me and said, "Miss Rushe wants a report."

I picked up the telephone. Georgia Rushe said, "Do you have anything to add to Mrs. Cool's information, Mr. Lam?"

"I think so," I said.

"What?"

I said, "You say the present Mrs. Crail was formerly Irma Begley, and she got acquainted with Ellery Crail through an automobile accident?"

"That's right."

"Crail struck her car?"

"Yes."

"She sustain personal injuries?"

"Yes. A spinal injury."

"Think she really has it?"

"It seems to have been definitely authenticated by X-rays."

I said, "Well, she probably got it a year or so earlier in another automobile accident. If we could prove that, would that mean anything to you?"

"Would it!" she said ecstatically.

"Well, don't get excited about it, and don't try any amateur detective work. Let us handle it."

"You're sure about this other automobile accident?" she asked.

"No, of course not. It's simply a lead."

"How long will it take you to find out?"

I said, "It depends upon when I can locate the other party to the accident, a man named Philip E. Cullingdon, and find out what he says."

"How long will it take you to do that?"

"I don't know. I'm starting on it right away."

She said, "I'll be waiting to hear from you, Mr. Lam. You folks have my telephone number up there. Call me at once in case you find anything. At once, please."

"Okay, I'll let you know," I said, and hung up.

All of a sudden Bertha began chuckling.

"Why the amusement?" I asked.

Bertha said, "I'm thinking of the way that little strumpet bawled me out when she went past, and then came back with that sickly sweet smile when she wanted me to be a witness for her. And I'm also thinking of the sweet time she'll have when she goes messing out around the address I gave her in Glendale trying to find a woman by the name of Boskovitche."

Chapter Five

NO ETCHINGS

PHILIP E. CULLINGDON turned out to be a middle-aged man with tired gray eyes from which spread a network of fine wrinkles. There were calipers around the edge of his mouth, and a certain firmness about the jaw. He gave the impression of being a kindly, somewhat quizzical man who would be slow to anger, but who could really go to town if he was once aroused.

I didn't beat around the bush any with him at all. I said, "You're Philip E. Cullingdon, the general contractor who was the defendant in the case of Begley versus Cullingdon?"

The tired gray eyes sized me up. "What's that to you?"

"I'm checking up on the case."

"What about it? It was all settled."

"Sure it was. You carried insurance, didn't you?"

"Yes."

"Do you know the amount of the settlement?"

"I know the amount of the settlement, but I still don't know to whom I'm talking, or why you want to know."

I handed him a card. "Donald Lam," I said, "of the firm of Cool & Lam, private investigators, and we're checking up on the case."

"For whom?"

"A client."

"Why?"

"I'm trying to find out something about Irma Begley, the plaintiff in the action."

"What about her?"

"I want to find out about the nature and extent of her injury."

He said, "I guess she was injured all right. The doctors say she was—doctors on both sides. Somehow, I never felt right about that case."

"What about it?"

He scratched his head.

I did a little prompting. I said, "I notice from the complaint that it was filed just about eleven months after the date of the accident. Were any previous demands made on you?"

Cullingdon said, "No. That's because the woman didn't think she was injured at first, didn't think it was anything serious. She had a little trouble, I guess, which gradually got worse. She went to a doctor who gave her some routine treatments and didn't think much of it; then finally she went to a specialist who told her she'd developed a complication from an injury she'd sustained —an injury to the spine."

"And that went back to the automobile accident?"

He nodded.

"So then she got some attorneys and sued you?"

Again he nodded.

"And your insurance company made a settlement?"

"That's right."

"At your suggestion?"

"As a matter of fact," Cullingdon said, "I was quite a bit put out about that. I didn't want the insurance company to settle it—not for any big sum."

"Why not?"

"Well, I didn't think it was my fault."

"Why?"

"Well, it was just one of those things. I thought she was a lot more to blame than I was. I'll admit I was trying to beat a signal, and I may have squeezed through a little bit, but just the same she was as much to blame as I was. Of course, the way it looked at first, no great damage was done. We busted a couple of headlights, crumpled a fender or two, and punched a hole in my radiator. She jumped out of the car as spry as you please, and I thought I was in for a tongue lashing, but she just laughed and said, 'Naughty, naughty, you shouldn't try to beat a signal.' "

"What did you say?"

"I told her, 'Naughty, naughty, you shouldn't go through an intersection at forty miles an hour.'"

"Then what?"

"Oh, we took each other's license numbers and exchanged cards, and a few people came up and gave advice, and then someone kept yelling to get the intersection cleaned up, and that was about all there was to it."

"Make any settlement with her?"

"She never submitted a bill."

"You didn't submit a bill to her?"

"No, I kept waiting, thinking something might come of it. Then when nothing did—well, to tell you the truth, I had just about forgotten about it when the action was filed."

"How much did the insurance company pay?"

"I don't know as they'd like to have me tell."

"Why not?"

"Well, it's—well, it was a good round figure. Apparently she really had a spinal injury."

"I'd like to know how much."

He said, "I'll tell you what I'll do. I'll ring up my insurance people tomorrow and ask them if there's any objection. If there isn't, I'll telephone your office and let you know how much it was."

"Will you tell me who carried your insurance?"

He smiled and shook his head. "I think I've told you about all I want to—going at it blind this way."

I said, "It's an interesting case."

"What interests me," Cullingdon said, "is what you're investigating. Do you think there was something fishy about it?"

I said, "Don't get that idea through your head. I might be just checking up on her general financial responsibility."

"Oh, I see," he said. "Well, I'll tell you, Mr. Lam, unless she spent that money foolishly, she should be a pretty good credit risk for anything within reason. She got a nice settlement out of the insurance company."

"Thanks," I told him. "You get in touch with them tomorrow, and give our office a ring and tell us how much it was—in case there's no objection. Will you?"

"Okay, sure."

We shook hands. I went down to the agency car and was just switching on the ignition when I saw another car pull up to the curb behind me and stop.

The young woman who got out of that car was a slender-waisted, smooth-hipped, easy moving package of class. I looked at her twice. Then I recognized her.

She was the girl who sold cigars and cigarettes at the Rimley Rendezvous.

I switched off the ignition on my car, lit a cigarette, and waited.

It was about a five-minute wait.

The girl came out, walking rapidly, pulled open the door of her car and jumped in.

I got out of my car and raised my hat with something of a flourish.

She waited while I walked over to stand beside the door of her car. "You have to have a license for that, you know," I said.

"For what?"

"For acting as private detective."

She flushed and said, "You certainly do get around, don't you?"

"So so. Not half as much as I should have."

"What do you mean by that?"

I said, "I'm a dumbbell when it comes to being a private dick."

"Looking at it from my angle, you don't seem to be dumb."

"I am."

"Just why?"

I said, "The county clerk's office is closed now."

"Well?"

I said, "I thought I was smart. I checked back on the Register of Actions, found where Irma Begley had been the plaintiff in a suit to recover damages from an automobile accident, and thought I'd done something smart."

"Hadn't you?"

"No."

"Why?"

"Because I quit."

"I don't get you."

I said, "As soon as I found where she had been a plaintiff in one suit, I made a note of the name of the defendant, the attorneys for the plaintiff, and walked out."

"What should you have done?"

"Kept on looking."

"You mean—"

"Of course I do." I grinned at her. "I'm hoping you weren't as dumb."

"Why?"

I said, "We can pool information and it will save me going to the county clerk's office tomorrow."

She said, "You're smart, aren't you?"

"I'm just telling you I'm dumb."

She said, "There are four actions that I know of."

"All under her own name?"

"Of course. She's not crazy that way."

"How did she really get the spinal injury?"

"I don't know."

"How long have you been checking on it?"

"I— Some little time."

"Why?"

She said, "You ask a lot of questions, don't you?"

I said, "Are you going to ride with me in my car? Am I going to ride with you in your car? Or have I got to follow you to see where you're going and what you do next?"

She thought that over for a moment then said, "If you're going any place with me, you're going in my car."

I was careful to walk around the front of the car so she couldn't start out without running over me, opened the door on the right-hand side, slid into the seat behind her, pulled the door shut, and said, "Okay, drive carefully because I'm always nervous with a strange driver."

She hesitated for a matter of seconds, then accepted the situation. "Do you," she asked bitterly, "*always* get what you start after?"

I smiled and said, "You'll feel better if I say yes, won't you?"

"I don't give a damn what you say," she said angrily.

"That simplifies it," I told her, and kept quiet.

After a while she said, "Well, what do you want, and where are we going?"

"You're driving the car," I told her. "And I want to know all the answers."

"Such as what?"

"What are your hours at the Rendezvous?"

She jerked her face around in surprise. The car wobbled on the road. She snapped her attention back to the car, said, "Well, of *all* the questions."

I didn't say anything.

She said, "I go on at twelve-fifteen. I'm supposed to be dressed, or undressed, whichever you want to call it, and on the floor by twelve-thirty. I work until four o'clock, then I come back at eight-thirty and work until midnight."

"You know Mrs. Ellery Crail?"

"Of course."

"Why the 'of course'?"

"She's there a great deal."

"Do you know the man who was with her this afternoon?"

"Yes."

"Now then," I said, "we begin to get into the big-money questions. Why were you interested in checking up on Mrs. Crail's past?"

"Just as a matter of curiosity."

"Your own curiosity, or the curiosity of someone else?"

"Mine."

"Are you that curious about all people?"

"No."

"Why this particular curiosity about Mrs. Crail?"

"I wondered about her—how she got her start."

"We wouldn't, by any chance, be going around in circles, would we?"

"What do you mean?"

"I asked you why you're checking up on her. It's curiosity. I asked you why the curiosity. You say it's because you wondered how she got her start. All of those words mean just about the same thing. Let's try some new meanings for a while."

"I'm telling you the truth."

"Sure you are. What I'm interested in is the reason back of the curiosity."

She drove along for a while apparently debating how much to tell me, then abruptly said, "What did you find out from Cullingdon?"

I said, "He wasn't suspicious when I called on him. He was interested, and he was going to ring his insurance people and find out if it was all right to tell me the amount of the settlement. I suppose after you talked with him he thought things were coming pretty fast."

"He did."

"What did he tell you?"

"He asked me questions about where I lived, and what my name was, and why I wanted to know."

"And you lied to him?"

"Oh, certainly. I told him I was a newspaper woman getting material for a feature story on certain types of automobile accidents."

"And he asked you what paper?"

Her face colored. "Yes."

"And then rang up the city desk?"

"How bright you are!"

"Did he?"

"Yes."

"And that was when you walked out?"

She nodded.

I said, "Well, the fat's in the fire now. If you hadn't called there, it's a ten to one shot he'd have called me, and told me the amount of—"

"What were *you* after?" she asked.

"The amount of the settlement."

She made a little deprecatory gesture. "The amount of the settlement," she said, "was seventeen thousand, eight hundred and seventy-five dollars."

It was my turn to look surprised. "What were *you* after?"

"Copies of the X-rays of the injuries, of course."

I thought for a minute then said, "I beg your pardon."

"What do you mean?"

"I mean that I'm sorry. I shouldn't have been so dumb. I had just learned about those other cases, and the full implications didn't dawn on me at once. I guess my mind's a little sluggish—a little out of practice."

"What'll the insurance company do?" she asked.

"They may start an independent check-up of their own."

There was savage triumph on her face. "That wouldn't make it so bad," she said, and then added, "if they did it soon enough."

I said, "You still haven't accounted for your curiosity."

"All right," she said angrily, "in case you're so damn dumb, which I don't think you are, Mrs. Crail was about to purchase the Stanberry Building, buying out old Rufus Stanberry."

I nodded.

"Well," she said, "use your head."

"You mean there's something in Rimley's lease about a purchase?"

"I believe so."

"In case of a bona fide sale the lease is terminated?"

"Within ninety days."

"And you're working for Rimley—getting a line on her so her hands will be tied?"

"In a way, yes."

"Just what's your connection with Rimley?"

"Is that a crack?"

"If you want to take it that way, yes."

She said, "Pittman Rimley is nothing to me, except in a business way, in case it's any of your business, which it isn't. But I own the hat-checking concession outright as well as the cigar, cigarette, and candy concessions."

"Do you have to work at them yourself?" I asked.

"I don't have to for financial reasons, if that's what you mean, but when you've got a business it's a lot better if you keep on the job yourself."

"You don't mind—the working conditions?"

"You mean the costume? Don't be silly. I have nice legs. If other people like to look at them, it's all right by me. I'm still the mistress of my own affections."

"You mean that after she bought the building, Rimley would have to negotiate another lease and that would enable him to either terminate your concessions or raise the ante?"

"Something of that sort."

"So Rimley knew about Irma Crail's past and gave you the information and told you to look it up, is that right?"

She hesitated a moment, then said, "Let's not talk about Rimley."

I let it go at that. "You say that Irma Crail had pulled this stuff before?"

"Several times."

"Where?"

"Once here, once in San Francisco, once in Nevada, and once in Nebraska."

"Using her own name each time? You're sure of that?"

"Yes."

"And how did *you* get this information?"

She shook her head.

I said, "All right, it's a reasonable inference that Rimley gave it to you. Now, let's go on from there. What was the name of this man you just called on?"

She frowned. "Covington."

I shook my head. "Cullingdon."

"Yes, that's right."

"You didn't remember it very well, did you?"

"I'm not so good at remembering names."

"In other words, you hadn't been familiar with the name for a very long time."

"What makes you say that?"

"Otherwise you'd have remembered it."

"I'm just not much good at names."

"Speaking of names?" I said and waited.

"You want my professional name or my real name?"

"Your real name," I said.

"I thought you would."

"Do I get it?"

"No."

"What's your professional name?"

"Billy Prue." She switched on the headlights.

"Nice name," I said. "It doesn't mean anything."

"Do names have to?"

"They should sound convincing."

"What does that sound like?"

"It sounds like a professional name—a stage name."

"Well, that's what it is. Therefore, it should be convincing."

"I suppose we could keep on arguing about that until you'd had sufficient opportunity to think up what you wanted to say about something else."

"*Will* you be quiet? I want to think."

"I thought that's what you wanted to do."

"All right, I do. I want to think something over."

"Cigarette?" I asked.

"No. Not while I'm driving," she added after a moment.

I settled down comfortably in the seat, cocked one elbow on the arm rest, and lit a cigarette.

We drove along for eight or ten blocks at almost a snail's pace, then suddenly she stepped on it.

"Well, that's something," I said.

"What?"

"That you've decided where we're going."

"I knew that all along—where *I* am going."

"Where's that?"

"To my apartment and change my clothes."

"And I take it the emphasis on the first person pronoun means that *my* ride terminates when we get to the apartment?"

"What did you want me to do," she asked, "adopt you?"

I grinned.

"I don't have any etchings if that's what you mean."

I didn't say anything.

She turned toward me, started to say something, checked herself, and remained silent.

After four or five minutes, she eased the car in to the curb. "It's been nice knowing you."

I said, "Don't bother, I'll wait."

"You'll have to wait a long time."

"That's all right."

"What are you waiting for?"

"Waiting to hear why you were so curious about Mrs. Crail."

"Well," she blazed angrily. "Sit there and wait then!"

She flounced out of the car, walked around behind the machine, took keys from her purse, latchkeyed the door of an apartment house, and went inside.

I was very careful not to turn my head, but by watching from the corner of my eye, I could see that she stopped after a few steps and remained standing there in the dimly lit lobby. She stood there for one minute—two minutes. Then she melted into the shadows and was gone.

Three minutes later and the door opened. A figure that clutched a fur coat tightly about her came running down the stairs toward the car.

I got out and started around politely to open the door. Cold fingers grabbed my wrists. "Come," she said in a hoarse whisper. "Please come—quick! Oh, my God!"

I started to ask her a question, then took another look at her face, changed my mind, and plodded along behind without a word.

The door had clicked shut, but she had the latchkey

in her right hand. Her left hand was clutching the coat about her.

She unlocked the door and walked through a lobby which was but little more than a wide place in a hallway, climbed three steps, walked down a carpeted corridor, entered an automatic elevator that wheezed and rattled up to the fourth floor.

She led the way down the corridor, paused before a door on the left. Once more her latchkey clicked back a lock and she pushed the door open. The lights were all on.

It was a three-room apartment, if you classified a little kitchenette as a room. It was on the street side and cost money.

Her purse, gloves, and the jacket she had been wearing lay on the table in the entrance room. There was an ash tray on that table with a single cigarette about half smoked. Through an open doorway I glimpsed a bedroom, and on the bed saw the skirt and blouse she had been wearing.

She followed the direction of my eyes, said in a hoarse whisper, "I was just changing my clothes—getting ready to take a bath. I flung on the first thing I could find to cover me up."

I looked again at the fur coat.

The left hand that was clutching it had puckered up a bit of the coat. Through it I could see the pink of satiny flesh.

"What's the rest of it?" I asked.

Wordlessly she crossed over to the door of the bathroom, then hung back.

"Please," she said, "you do it."

I opened the door and looked inside.

The bathroom light was on.

The body of the man who had escorted Mrs. Ellery Crail to the Rimley Rendezvous that afternoon was in the bathtub, the knees high up against the chest, the head back against the sloping end of the bathtub, the eyes about two-thirds closed, the lower jaw hanging limp leaving the mouth partially open.

Telling the girl to keep back out of the way and reaching for the lifeless wrist was only a mere formality.

Rufus Stanberry's heart was as still as a churchyard on a frosty morning.

Even in death, however, he had that shrewdly calculating leer on his face. The man might have been making an audit of eternity.

"He's—dead?" she asked from the doorway.

"He's dead," I said.

Chapter Six

WRONG ANSWERS

WE WENT BACK TO THE BEDROOM. She was shaking with nervousness.

I said, "Sit down. We have a little talking to do."

"I don't know a thing about it," she said. "You know as well as I do that I wasn't up here long enough to—"

I said, "Let's let that go and start with facts. What happened?"

"I've already told you. I came in here and started to undress. I headed for the bathroom, switched on the lights, and—and—"

"You switched on the bathroom light?" I asked.

"Yes."

"You're sure it wasn't on already?"

"No. I switched it on, and then I saw him and—well, I just ran back and grabbed the first thing I could throw around me and ran down to get you."

"Pretty much of a panic?"

"What do you mean?"

"You were frightened?"

"Of course."

"You didn't know he was here?"

"No, I—"

"Take another look."

"I—"

"Go ahead. Look."

I pushed her over to the bathroom door. She grabbed at the side of the door. The coat fell open. She had on a bra, panties, and dark lustrous stockings. She gave a short, sharp exclamation and kept clinging to the side of the door, not bothering about the coat. "Take a *good* look," I said.

She said, "What is there to see? Just a dead man in a bathroom."

She twisted out of my grasp, darted back to the bedroom.

I carefully closed the bathroom door. "Where's the telephone?"

"Right there."

"Oh, yes," I said. I sat down and took one of the packages of cigarettes she had sold me that afternoon from my pocket, shook a cigarette a third of the way out, extended it to her, "Smoke?"

"No, I—"

I took the cigarette from the pack, tapped it on my thumbnail, put it in my mouth, lit it, and settled back in the chair.

"The telephone," she said. "It's right there."

I nodded.

"Aren't you going to call the police?"

"Not yet."

"Why?"

"I'm waiting."

"For what?"

"For you."

"What about me?"

"To think up a better story."

"What do you mean?"

I said, "The police won't believe that story of yours. That will make it bad—for you."

A hot flash of anger crossed her face. "What do you mean?"

I inhaled cigarette smoke and slowly exhaled it.

"If you don't call the police, *I'll* call them," she threatened.

There were magazines on the table. I picked up one, settled back in the chair, and started turning the pages, looking at the pictures. "Go ahead."

The silence lasted for ten or fifteen seconds, then she moved toward the telephone. "I'm not kidding. If you're not going to call the police, I'll call them."

I kept turning the pages of the magazine.

She picked up the telephone receiver, started to dial,

looked back at me, and then slammed the receiver back into place. "What's wrong with my story?"

"Two or three things."

"Bosh!"

"One thing," I said, "that the police will notice. A couple of other things they won't."

"What's the thing the police will notice?"

"The thing that proves you're lying."

"I don't like the way you're saying that."

"I don't like the way I have to say it."

"All right, if you're so smart, tell me what's wrong with my story."

I pointed to her purse on the table.

"What about it?"

"Your keys were in that purse."

"Naturally."

"How many keys do you have?"

She showed me the leather key container with its open zipper. There were four keys on the inside.

I said, "All right, you took out your keys downstairs. You opened the zipper, selected the key to your apartment. I take it that key opens the spring lock on the door downstairs?"

She nodded.

I said, "You kept the key out because you wanted to enter your apartment. You came up here and entered your apartment. Then what did you do?"

"I'm telling you I started to change my clothes and—"

I said, "The natural thing was to have closed the zipper and dropped the key container back into your purse."

"Well, I— Well, certainly. That's what I did. Good Heavens! I didn't have to tell you every single solitary move I made, did I? I put the keys back in the purse, put the purse on the table. I walked across to the bedroom. I switched on the bedroom lights. I was undressing before I'd made two steps in the bedroom. I kicked off my skirt. I went to the bathroom. I opened the door of the bathroom—"

"Go on from there."

"I switched on the lights and saw that man and didn't even stop to take a good look at him. I dashed down—"

"Did you know he was dead?"

"No, of course not. I wasn't certain but what he might have been waiting for me."

"To harm you?"

"Well, yes—or perhaps—"

I said, "They make passes at a girl in your position?"

"Don't be silly, they make passes at attractive women in any position."

"Most men think you're easy because you wander around and show your legs?"

"It's a natural assumption, isn't it? You can't blame them too much."

"They follow you to your apartment?"

"They have."

"Try to date you up occasionally?"

"Of course."

"How did you know this wasn't a Johnny who had staked himself out?"

"I didn't."

"Then you thought that when I opened the door I might have a battle on my hands."

"I didn't know."

"You didn't say anything."

"I wanted you to see—what I'd seen."

I shook my head and said, "You knew he was dead."

"Is that the point in my story you say the police will disbelieve?"

"No."

"What is it?"

"Your key, and your purse."

"What about it?"

I said, "According to your story, you were in a panic. You had on a bra and panties. You grabbed up a fur coat, wrapped it around you, and dashed downstairs to call me. That doesn't fit with the facts. If you'd put your keys back in the purse and put the purse on the table and really *were* in a panic, you certainly wouldn't have stopped to open the purse, take out the keys, put the purse back on the table, and then run down to find me. You'd have grabbed up the purse and looked for the keys after you'd got downstairs."

"And that's it?" she asked somewhat scornfully.

"That's it," I said quietly. "The fact that you had the key to the apartment in your hand when you came downstairs showed that you knew you were going to have to use it."

"Certainly; I knew I was going to have to use it to get back into the apartment house and also into my apartment. There are spring locks and automatic door-closers on both doors."

I said, "And you knew you were going to have to use it. That's why you kept it in your hand, why you went in and tossed the purse on the table. Then you went into the bedroom, tossed the keys over on the bed, slipped out of your skirt, blouse, and jacket, wrapped up in the fur coat, popped your head in the bathroom to make sure the body was still there, then grabbed the keys and ran down the stairs."

"Phooey!" she said scornfully, picked up the telephone again and said, "Now I'll dial Police Headquarters."

"And on that pillow," I said, "which is a very soft one, you can see the place where the keys landed when you tossed them onto the bed."

"Why, I—" She dropped the telephone receiver, jumped up and ran to the door of the bedroom, looked inside, and then came out saying scornfully, "What a smart detective *you* are. The bed is covered with a bedspread that completely covers the pillows. Even if I'd thrown the keys on the pillows there wouldn't have been enough indentation through that heavy bedspread to have let you see what it was."

"That's right."

"Then what did you mean by saying there was an indentation there?"

I said, "If you'd actually been telling the truth and

the keys had been in your purse all the time, you wouldn't have rushed to the door in a panic to see if there actually was an indentation there."

She thought that over for a moment, then sat down.

I said, "So much for the police. From my own viewpoint, there are other things that don't check. You were anxious to let me see that you had on just panties and a bra under the fur coat so as to give authenticity to your story. And you were very suddenly in a great dither to find out something about Irma Crail—something that you could use as actual proof in case you had to, and you were trembling all over when you came out of Cullingdon's apartment. You were so nervous you could hardly shift the gears in your automobile. The way I put that together, you came home this afternoon, took off your clothes, went to the bathroom, saw the body of Rufus Stanberry in the tub, convinced yourself he was dead, sat down and thought for a moment, smoked that one cigarette about half through (the one single long stub with the red lipstick on it in this ash tray), put your clothes back on and went out, being very, very careful to leave absolutely nothing which indicated you'd already been in your apartment and discovered the body. You overlooked the cigarette.

"Then you went to Cullingdon's in very much of a hurry. You'd found I'd been there and that upset your plans. I picked you up as you came out, and that bothered you still more. You sparred for time while you were doing some thinking—you needed some witness to show that you had entered your apartment innocently and this dead man was occupying your bathtub. After all, why wouldn't I be a better witness than someone you'd pick up to back your play. I'd be sincere and disinterested. I'd tell a story the police would believe. So you elected me as the fall guy. You drove up to the apartment house. You got out with your key in your hand. You went upstairs. You put the key down on the bed, leaving your open purse on the table in the other room. You jumped out of your skirt and blouse, put the fur coat on, gave a quick look to see everything was as you'd left it in the bathroom and then came down and pulled your act on me. You thought I'd fall for it, telephone the police and vouch that you'd gone up to your apartment, hadn't been gone more than two or three minutes and—"

She said wearily, "All right, what do you want? Give me a cigarette."

I gave her a cigarette. "I want the truth," I said.

"All right, it happened just about the way you thought it did. I didn't realize the keys would betray me."

"You found him here just before you went out to see Cullingdon?"

"Yes."

"Know who he was?"

"Of course."

"Found out he was dead?"

"Yes."

"And did what?"

"Naturally, I thought Mrs. Crail was playing me for a fall guy. He'd been with her. Now he was in my apartment—dead. I didn't like the smell of it. No one could prove I'd been here. I decided to go out, get what I could on Mrs. Crail, and then go to see her and call for a showdown—or else pick up some witness who could come to the apartment with me and—well, sort of give me an alibi. Then you showed up and, while I was annoyed at first, I finally decided you'd be a good witness."

I said, "You're not going to like my next question."

"What is it?"

I jerked my head toward the bathroom. "He ever been here before?"

She met my eyes. "Yes."

"Social or sexual?"

"Neither."

"No passes?"

"That wasn't what he came for."

"But he did make passes?"

"He tried an awkward, clumsy approach, just to see

if it would get him anywhere. He seemed almost relieved when he found out it wouldn't."

"What did he want?"

"Wanted to find out whether Rimley was doing a good enough business to stand for a boost in rent."

"Did he find out anything?"

"Not a thing."

I said, "Let's go take another look at that body."

"We aren't supposed to touch it, are we, until—?"

"No," I said.

We went back through the bedroom and into the bathroom. She was calmly practical now, with no trace of panic in her manner.

As well as I could without disturbing the body, I looked it over. Evidently he had been killed by a single hard blow on the left temple with some object that had left an oblong depressed fracture of the skull. I looked in the right-hand inside pocket of the coat. There was a billfold in there. It was filled with folding money, lots of it. I put it back. The side pocket on the left held a notebook. On the front page the words had been written in pen and ink, *Rufus Stanberry, 3271 Fulrose Avenue. In case of accident notify Archie Stanberry, 963 Malolo Avenue. My blood type is 4.* I closed the book, slipped it back in the pocket.

I saw an expensive wrist watch on his left wrist. I looked at the time. It was five thirty-seven.

I consulted my own watch.

The time was exactly six thirty-seven.

That did it. I backed away from the body as though it had had leprosy.

"What's the matter?" she asked, watching me. "What's wrong with the watch?"

"Nothing," I said, and took her out to the other room. "It's all right. We call the police now."

Chapter Seven

BERTHA SMELLS MONEY

THE TWO OFFICERS FROM THE RADIO PROWL CAR who got there first to hold things in line until Homicide could arrive asked only a few sketchy questions. Then Homicide showed up and we told our stories. Nothing else happened for about an hour, then Sergeant Frank Sellers came strolling in, his hat on the back of his head, a soggy cigar half chewed to ribbons in the side of his mouth.

"Hello, Donald," he said. "Damn glad to see you're back."

We shook hands. I introduced him to the girl.

They'd taken our stories down in shorthand. Sellers had evidently had a transcript and familiarized himself with it before he arrived on the scene.

He said, "Too bad that you had to come back and stick your nose into a murder case first rattle out of the box, Lam. As I gather it, you're working on a case?"

He jerked his head toward Billy Prue. "Business or social?"

"Confidentially, it's a little of both. That's not for the press—and it's not for Bertha."

He looked Billy Prue over, said, "Now as I understand it, she parked her car down in front and went up to change her clothes."

"That's right," she said in a low voice.

"You two were going out to dinner?"

I nodded.

"She didn't know you well enough to invite you in," Sellers said, "and she didn't want to keep you waiting very long, so she was in a hurry?"

Billy Prue said, with a nervous little laugh, "I was undressing almost before I'd got through the door. I started for the bathroom and—and found that."

"What did you do with your keys when you came in?" Sellers asked casually.

"Put them in my purse," she said, "and dropped the purse on the table."

"And when you ran out, what did you do—take the keys out of the purse?"

She met his eyes steadily. "Certainly not. I grabbed up the whole purse, tucked it under my arm, and dashed out of the place. Then after I got Donald to come back with me, I opened my purse, took out my keys, and unlocked the door."

Sergeant Sellers heaved a weary sigh. "Well, folks, I guess that's all. We may want to ask you some more questions later on. Guess you can go on out to dinner now."

"Thanks," I told him.

"How's Bertha these days?"

"Seems to be the same as ever," I said.

"Haven't seen her for a while. Well, now that you're back, I may see her more frequently."

His grin was maliciously significant.

Billy Prue asked, "Are the—are the police through here?"

"Not yet," Sellers said. "Don't worry, everything will be all right. You've got your keys, haven't you?"

"Yes."

"All right, run along to dinner and have a good time."

Sergeant Sellers stayed in the apartment, watched us from the doorway as we walked down the corridor to the automatic elevator.

"Well," Billy Prue said with a sigh as we entered the elevator, "that's that."

I pushed the button for the ground floor. "No talking," I warned.

The elevator rattled to a stop. A plain-clothes man on guard in the lower corridor passed us through with a nod. There was a uniformed officer on duty at the doorway. Billy Prue's car was parked where we had left it. There was white dust on the steering-wheel and the door catches where the police had gone over it for fingerprints. Aside from that, it was exactly as we had left it.

Without a word, I opened the door of the car. She got in with a swift all-of-a-sudden grace and with a twist of her supple body, adjusted herself behind the steering-wheel. I slid in the seat beside her and slammed the door shut.

We moved away from the curb.

"All right, sucker," she said.

I didn't say anything.

"You stuck your neck out," she said. "You're in it as deep as I am now, and you've got nothing further on me. You can't say a word without getting yourself in bad."

"So what?"

"So," she said, "I do you the extreme courtesy of taking you back to where you left your automobile—that is, if you're nice. Otherwise, I'd dump you out on the street."

"Rather a hard-boiled attitude when I've stuck my neck out to help you, isn't it?"

"That," she said, "is what you get for being a sucker."

I leaned back against the cushions, took a cigarette package from my pocket, shook out one. "Cigarette?" I asked.

"Not while I'm driving."

I lit one and smoked, watching her profile.

Her eyes blinked rapidly two or three times. Then I saw a tear come out and trickle down her cheek.

"What's the matter?" I asked.

She drove the car with a certain savage carelessness at an increasing speed.

"Nothing."

I kept on smoking.

She turned a corner. I saw we were headed for the Stanberry Building and apparently the Rimley Rendezvous.

"Change your mind about taking me back to where my car is?"

"Yes."

"Why are you crying?"

She pulled in to the curb, slammed the car to a stop, groped in her purse, pulled out some cleansing tissue and wiped her eyes. "You make me so damn mad," she said.

"Why?"

"I wanted to see what you'd do. I pulled that gag on you that you'd been a sucker just to see what happened."

"Well?"

"Nothing happened, damn you. You took it for granted that I was right. You thought I was the kind that would do a trick like that, didn't you?"

"That's what you said."

"You should have known I was trying to get a rise out of you."

I watched her clean up the traces of her tears. "I'd kill myself before I'd do anything like that for a man who befriended me. Darn few of them have ever taken the trouble, unless they wanted something very obviously and very immediately."

I still didn't say anything.

She flashed me one look still hot with hurt and anger. Then she snapped her purse shut, adjusted herself in the driver's seat with a quick angry flounce and started driving again.

We stopped in front of the Stanberry Building.

I said, "Pittman Rimley doesn't like me."

"You don't need to go in. I've got to report. You can wait here."

"And then?"

"Then I'll drive you out to where you left your car."

I thought that over. "Going to tell Rimley I was with you when you notified the police?"

"Yes. I'll have to do that."

I said, "Go on up. I'll wait if it isn't too long. If it is, I'll grab a cab. Better lock your car just in case."

She looked at me sharply, then locked the ignition. "Some day," she warned, "I'm going to jar you out of that detached, don't-give-a-damn pose."

I waited until she was inside, then got out and looked for a taxi. If I'd been parking in a taxi zone one would have whizzed up inside of ten seconds. As it was, I waited ten minutes, then started walking down the avenue. I'd gone five blocks before I found one.

I got in, gave the address of Cullingdon's place where I'd left the agency car. I paid off the cab, started the agency heap, and drove to the office—fast.

The office was dark when I arrived.

I called Bertha's apartment. She didn't answer. I sat down in the dark to do a little thinking.

After about ten minutes, I heard the pound of heavy steps in the corridor. A latchkey jabbed the door. The lock clicked back and Bertha Cool flung the door open.

"Where the hell have *you* been?" she asked.

"Places."

She glowered at me.

"Had dinner?" I asked.

"Yes."

"I haven't."

Bertha heaved herself into a chair. "When it comes time to eat, I eat. I've got a big dynamo running and it takes fuel to keep it going."

I shook the last cigarette out of the package, crumpled it, and dropped it in the ash tray.

"Well, we've run slap bang into a murder case."

"A murder!"

I nodded.

Bertha said, "Who was bumped off?"

"Rufus Stanberry."

"Where? How? Why?"

I said, "The place was the apartment of the cigarette girl who works at the Rimley Rendezvous. Her stage name is Billy Prue. As to the how, the process was very primitive and very simple. It consisted of hitting the man a very hard blow on the temple. It's the why that complicates things."

"Well, what's your best guess?"

"Either the man knew too much, or—"

"Or what?" Bertha snapped as I paused. "Go ahead."

"Or," I said, "he knew too little."

Bertha glowered at me. "Just like one of those news commentators," she snorted. "You state the perfectly obvious, so it sounds profound as hell."

I devoted my attention to smoking.

After a minute Bertha said, "You do get the agency into the damnedest things."

"I didn't get the agency into it," I said.

"You may think you didn't, but you did, just the same. I'd have handled this case, and it would have turned out to be nothing beyond the little routine job of checking back on a woman's record, finding nothing that would have been of any benefit to our client, and—"

"The minute you started to check," I said, "you'd have found something that would have been of the greatest interest to our client—something about Mrs. Crail."

"What?"

I said, "She's a professional malingerer."

"What have you got on her?"

"Some of it's hearsay. There's a case of Begley versus Cullingdon. Going back a while before that, I understand there are other cases in San Francisco and in Nevada."

"Fakes or injuries?" Bertha asked.

"No, that fake stuff is too risky. She suffered an injury all right, probably in the first accident, found out how easy it was to collect and decided it was easier than working for a living. She'd wait for an opportunity to have just the right sort of accident, one where she didn't stand too much chance of getting busted up. She could tell the insurance company representative very bravely that she had just been shaken up a little; that she didn't want a cent—goodness no! It wasn't her fault, of course, but her injuries weren't enough to bother about. Then after the lapse of a few months, she'd go to a doctor and complain of symptoms, then recall she'd been in an automobile accident, although she'd almost forgotten about it. The doctor would send her to a lawyer, then there'd be a great hubbub. It would seem that she'd suffered a spinal injury and thought at the time she'd just jarred a rib loose and it would heal right up."

"Couldn't they catch her at it?"

"Not very well. She'd wait until just before the expiration of the statute of limitations before she'd file suit. X-rays would show she had an injury. She's an attractive girl. She could do things in front of a jury. Insurance companies would settle. Cosgate & Glimson handled her last case."

"Why did she quit it?"

"Because it got too risky. She'd done it several times, and insurance companies have a way of comparing notes on those things. In all probability, she didn't intend to use the same racket to get herself a husband because, obviously, she couldn't tell by the way a man was driving a car whether he'd make a good matrimonial catch. But when she had this accident with Crail's car—well, it developed Crail was a good matrimonial catch, so she did her stuff."

Bertha said, "Well, we've done two hundred dollars worth of work for our client. Stall around for a couple of days picking up the record on these other cases, then we'll put the information in the hands of Miss Georgia Rushe and let her handle Mrs. Crail any way she damn pleases. We'll just check out of it and keep from getting mixed up in that murder. You *aren't* mixed up in it, are you, lover?"

"No."

"I'm beginning to think you are."

"What makes you think so?"

"The way you say you aren't. Is there a girl in it?"

"Not in it. He was found in this girl's apartment."

"You say it was the cigarette girl?"

"Yes."

"The one who sold you three packages of cigarettes?"

"That's right."

"Humph," Bertha said, then suddenly swung her head around to let her eyes glitter into mine. "Legs?"

"Naturally."

"I mean pretty?"

"Very."

"Humph," Bertha said, then after a moment added, "Now you listen to me, Donald Lam, you keep out of this, and—"

Knuckles sounded on the door of the office.

I said to Bertha, "Call out through the door that you're closed up."

Bertha said, "Don't be silly. Perhaps it's a client with money."

I said, "I can see her outline through the frosted glass. It's a woman."

"All right, then, perhaps it's a woman with money."

Bertha marched across to the door, shot back the bolt, and pulled the door open.

A young woman on the threshold smiled up at Bertha.

She looked like a million dollars net with a fur coat and a big collar that came up to frame her face. She carried her own Dun & Bradstreet rating on her back, the sort of client who can really finance an investigation.

Bertha Cool's manner melted like a chocolate bar in a kid's fist. "Come in," she said, "come in! We're closed, but since you've taken the trouble to come up here, we'll see you."

"May I ask your name, please?" our visitor asked Bertha.

I could see Bertha looking at the girl with a slight frown as though she might have seen her before, or was trying to place her.

"I'm Bertha Cool," Bertha said, "one of the partners in this agency, and this is Donald Lam, the other partner. Now you're Miss—Miss—Miss—"

"Witson," the young woman beamed. "Miss Esther Witson."

"Oh, yes," Bertha said.

"I wanted to talk with you, Mrs. Cool, about—"

"Go ahead," Bertha said, "talk right here. Mr. Lam and myself are at your service. Anything we can do for you—"

Miss Witson turned large blue eyes at me. Her lips slid back along prominent teeth to show how pleased she was.

Bertha recognized her then. "Fry me for an oyster!" Bertha exclaimed. "You're the woman who was driving the automobile."

"Why, yes, Mrs. Cool, I thought you knew. I had quite a time finding you. You remember you gave the name of Boskovitche." And Miss Witson threw back her head and let the light gleam on a whole mouthful of horse teeth.

Bertha looked at me with an expression of trapped, exasperated helplessness on her face.

"There's some dispute about responsibility for the accident is there, Miss Witson?" I asked.

She said, "That's a mild way of expressing it."

"No serious damages, are there?" Bertha chimed in.

"That's a mild way of describing it."

"Just what do you mean?" Bertha demanded.

She said, "The other car was driven by a Mr. Rolland B. Lidfield. His wife was riding in the car with him."

"But the cars weren't badly damaged, were they?"

"It isn't the cars," Miss Witson explained. "It's Mrs. Lidfield. She claims she suffered a severe nervous shock and she's placed herself in the hands of her physician, leaving her husband to do the talking for her—her husband and her lawyers."

"Lawyers!" Bertha exclaimed. "So soon!"

"A firm of attorneys who specialize in that sort of thing, I understand—Cosgate & Glimson. The doctor got them."

I glanced at Bertha to see if the name registered.

It didn't.

"Cosgate and—what was that other name?" I asked.

"Cosgate & Glimson."

I glanced at Bertha, slowly closed my left eye.

"Humph!" Bertha said.

"I wanted you to help me out, Mrs. Cool."

"In what way?"

"Telling what happened."

"It was just another automobile smashup," Bertha said, glancing uneasily at me.

"But you know that I was driving very slowly; that I was behind your car for two or three blocks; that you slowed down almost to a snail's pace and I went around you—"

"I don't know any such thing," Bertha said.

"And," Miss Witson went on triumphantly, "*you* tried to get out of it by giving an assumed name when we wanted you as a witness. That won't do you any good, Mrs. Cool, because I took down the number of your car. And I guess the only reason I did that is because I saw Mr. Lidfield writing down the numbers of all the cars that were near by. So they'll call you for a witness anyway, which, after all, Mrs. Cool, means that you'll have to take one side or the other. You'll have to make up your mind which car was in the wrong."

Bertha said, "There's nothing for me to make up my mind about. I don't have to take sides with anyone."

"There were some other witnesses?" I asked Miss Witson.

"Oh, yes."

"Who were they?"

"Lots of them. A Mr. Stanberry, a Mrs. Crail, two or three others."

I said to Bertha, "That would make it very, very interesting—hearing what Mrs. Crail would have to say on the witness stand about that."

Bertha's jaw pushed forward. She said, "Well, I can tell you one thing. The car that whipped around to the left was going like a bat out of hell. He saw that Stanberry's car was going to turn to the left, so he thought there was a chance for him to cut his own car sharp to the left and go through all the other traffic."

Miss Witson nodded and said, "I had the right of way

on him. I was the first one in the intersection. I was on his right, and he was coming from my left, so I had every right to keep right on going—the right of way, you know."

Bertha nodded.

"And," Miss Witson went on triumphantly, "I didn't hit him at all. He's the one who hit me. You can see from the marks on the car that he ran right smack into me."

Bertha was suddenly friendly. "All right, dearie. I wouldn't worry about it if I were you. The man was speeding across an intersection, and Mrs. Lidfield sounds to me like a gold digger."

Esther Witson impulsively gave Mrs. Cool her hand. "I'm *so* glad you feel that way about it, Mrs. Cool, and you don't need to worry about the time you put in being a witness. Of course, I can't make any *promise,* because that would look as though I were trying to buy your testimony. But I realize that you're a professional woman and that if this is going to take some of your time, well—" She smiled sweetly. "You know, I always *try* to be very fair in my business deals."

"Don't you," I asked abruptly, "carry insurance?"

Miss Witson laughed. "I thought I did, but it seems I didn't. I guess I was a little careless about that. Well, thank you ever so much, Mrs. Cool, and you can rest assured that— Well, you know, I can't say anything, but—"

She smiled significantly and wished us a good night.

Bertha sniffed the air. "That perfume," she said, "costs about fifty bucks an ounce. And did you notice that mink coat? That's what you have to do in a detective business, Donald darling. You have to establish contacts, particularly among the wealthy."

I said, "I thought you told me she was a buck-toothed, pop-eyed little bitch who—"

"She looks a lot different now," Bertha said with dignity.

Chapter Eight

ONE HUNDRED PERCENT RAT

THE PLACE I WANTED turned out to be a three-story brick apartment house with a stucco front. It didn't have a switchboard. The front door was kept locked with a spring catch, and there was a row of bell buttons with speaking-tubes and cards.

I'd picked out the name, *Stanberry, A. L.*, and pressed a button. After a few seconds, a speaking-tube emitted a shrill whistle. A moment later, a voice said, "What do you want?"

I put my mouth up to the speaking-tube. "Archie Stanberry."

"Who wants him?"

"My name's Lam."

"What do you want to see him about?"

"You guess."

"Newspaper?"

"What do you think?"

The buzzer sounded on the door, and I pushed it open and went in.

Archie Stanberry's apartment was 533. An automatic elevator that really moved whisked me up to the floor. I walked down to apartment 533 and tapped on the door.

Archie Stanberry was about twenty-five or twenty-six. His complexion was about the color of pie crust that should have been left in the oven another fifteen minutes. His eyes were swollen and red from crying, but he was trying to be brave. The apartment was swank and looked as though Archie had lived there for some time.

"It's been an awful shock to me," he said.

"Of course."

I didn't wait for an invitation, but walked on in calmly, picked out a comfortable chair, sat down, took out one of the packages of cigarettes Billy Prue had sold me, jiggled out a cigarette, lit it, said, "What's your relationship?"

"He was my uncle."

"See him frequently?"

"We were inseparable."

I pulled a notebook out of my pocket.

"When did you last see your uncle?"

"Yesterday night."

"Ever hear him speak of Billy Prue—the young woman who lived in the apartment where the body was found?"

"No."

"You didn't know that he knew her?"

"No."

"Know what he was doing there?"

"I don't," Archie said, "but I can assure you that whatever it was, it was something that was on the up-and-up. My uncle was a paragon of virtue."

He mouthed the words as though he'd been making a nominating speech.

"Lived here long?" I asked.

"Five years."

"Who owns the building?"

"Uncle Rufus."

"Left rather a considerable estate?"

He said almost too hastily, "I don't know. I know very little about his financial affairs. I've always gathered that he was affluent."

"You work?" I asked.

"At present," he said, "I am not working in the sense of having employment. I am doing research work for an historical novel."

"Ever had anything published?" I asked.

He flushed and said, "I don't think that needs to enter into it."

I said, "I thought you might like the publicity—that was all."

He said, "This is an idea for an historical novel that appealed to Uncle Rufus."

"He was financing it?" I asked.

For a minute the eyes avoided mine, then came back to look at me—bloodshot, restless eyes that seemed afraid of something. "Yes," he said, "and now I suppose I'll have to drop it."

"What's it about generally?"

"The Coast Guard."

"And historical?"

"Back to the days of the real Merchant Marine," he said with a note of enthusiasm coming into his voice. "Back when San Francisco was a real port, a real city that had ships from all corners of the world crowding in through the Golden Gate. Days that are past, but days that will come again when once more American merchandise begins to move in American bottoms, when you can stand on a headland anywhere along the coast and look out and see the smudge of smoke on the horizon, when—"

"Nice stuff," I interrupted. "Your uncle wasn't married?"

"No."

"Any other relatives?"

"None that I know of."

"Leave a will?"

"Really, Mr.—"

"Lam."

"Really, Mr. Lam, I don't see the pertinency of that question. May I ask what paper you're with?"

"None."

"What!"

"None."

"I understood you were gathering material for the press."

I said, "I'm a detective."

"Oh!" The exclamation was short and sharp.

"When did you hear about it?"

"About my uncle's death?"

"Yes."

"A very short time after the body was found I was

notified and asked to go over—to the apartment where the body was found."

"Nice place you have here," I said.

"I like it. I've told my uncle several times that I could get along in a smaller apartment, but he insists that I should have this. It's rather elaborate—two apartments merged into one."

He blew his nose again, abruptly said to me, "There's something in my right eye. Will you excuse me for a moment?"

"Yes."

"A little cinder or something," he said.

He twisted a handkerchief, moistened the end, went over to a mirror and pulled down the lid of his right eye.

"Perhaps I can help you," I said.

"Perhaps."

He rolled his right eye up. There was a little brownish speck down at the very bottom of the eye. I speared it with the handkerchief, and he said, "Thanks."

We went back to our chairs and sat down.

"Have you any clues as to—as to how it happened?" he asked.

I said, "I'm not with the police. I'm private."

"A private detective?"

"Right."

"May I ask who employed you, what your interest is, why you—" He stopped and looked at me.

I said, "I'm interested in a very incidental angle. I believe your uncle was about to sell the Stanberry Building."

"I think he was."

"Did he say anything to you about it?"

"Just generally. I knew that a sale was pending."

"Know what the price was?"

"I don't know, and if I did, I see no reason why I should communicate the information to you. After all, Mr. Lam, it seems to me that you're being rather impertinent in your inquiries."

"How old was your uncle?"

"Fifty-three."

"Ever been married?"

"Yes."

"Widower?"

"No. There was a divorce."

"How long ago?"

"About two years, I believe."

"You knew his wife?"

"Oh, yes, of course."

"Where is she now?"

"I don't know."

"Did she get the divorce, or did he?"

"She did."

"A property settlement?"

"I believe so, yes. Really, Mr. Lam, this is taking the inquiry very far afield, don't you think?"

"Did you tell the police any more than you told me?"

"I don't think I told them as much. Your questions are rather—rather personal."

"I'm sorry," I said. "You see, I—" I choked in mid-sentence, coughed, gagged, muttered, "Bathroom, quick!"

He ran to a door, opened it. I lurched through. He ran across the bedroom, opened the bathroom door. I went in, waited five seconds, then opened the door. I could hear his voice in the living-room. He was telephoning.

I took a quick look around the bedroom. It was neat and well kept. The closet was filled with clothes. A shoe shelf had nearly two dozen pairs of shoes all neatly treed. On the inside of the closet door were two necktie racks that must have held something over a hundred neckties. On the dressing-table, brushes and comb were neatly arranged. The brushes were clean and so was the comb. There were, perhaps, a dozen framed photographs on the dresser, or hanging on the walls. Directly across from the bed was an oval space measuring about twelve inches the long way, about eight inches the other, just a little different color from the rest of the wall. On the dresser, a cigarette had been torn in two, and both ends lay there. It was the only bit of litter in the room.

Abruptly the door opened. Archie Stanberry stood in the doorway looking at me reproachfully. "I thought you wanted to go to the bathroom?"

"I did. Nice place you have here."

"Mr. Lam, I'm going to have to ask you to leave. I don't like your methods."

"Okay by me," I said. I walked out to the sitting-room. Stanberry made something of a ceremony of moving across and flinging open the outer door, then standing in statuesque dignity.

I didn't go out. I walked back to the easy chair and sat down.

For a moment Stanberry maintained his pose. Then he said, "I'm asking you to leave. If you don't leave, I shall have to do something about it."

"Go ahead," I invited.

He waited, then slowly closed the door.

For a moment we looked at each other. Then Stanberry said, "I did you the extreme courtesy of permitting you to intrude upon my grief because I thought you were a gentleman of the press."

His tone was reproachfully cultured.

"I told you I'm a detective."

"Had you told me that earlier, I should not have admitted you—particularly had I known you were a *private* detective."

"A detective has to look around," I said.

"Mr. Lam, I don't know just what your game is, or what you're trying to do, but if you don't leave at once, I shall call the officers."

"Suits me," I said. "When you call them, call Frank Sellers. He's connected with Homicide. He's working on your uncle's death."

I sat there and Archie Stanberry stood there. After a moment, Stanberry walked dubiously to the telephone, then detoured and sat down. "I can't understand the reason for this rudeness," he said.

I said, "In the first place, while you are a meticulous

little man with neat habits, you aren't *that* neat." I jerked my thumb toward the bedroom. "You are the favorite nephew of a rich uncle who owns the joint. Therefore, you get maid service—and how. That bedroom of yours is as clean as a new pin."

"What's that got to do with it?" he asked.

I grinned and said, "That's the weak point in your armor."

"What do you mean?"

I put all the assurance in the world in my voice. "The maid," I said, "will be able to tell what picture was taken down from that wall—*that's* where you made your mistake. You shouldn't have taken down the whole frame. You should have pulled out the back of the frame, removed the picture, put in another one and hung the frame back in place. As it is, you can see a little difference in color where the frame was removed. And, of course, there's the little hole in the wall left by the steel pushpin that held the picture."

He looked at me as though I'd hit him in the stomach.

"So," I said, "go ahead and call the police. When Frank Sellers comes, we'll bring the maid in here and show her Billy Prue's picture and ask her if that's the one that was removed from the wall right across from your bed."

His shoulders sagged as though both lungs had gone flat.

"What—what do you want?"

"The truth, naturally."

"Lam, I'm going to tell you something I've never told anyone else—something that I've never expected to admit to a single soul."

I didn't say anything, but just sat there waiting.

He said, "I dropped in at the Rendezvous every once in a while. It's only natural that I should have."

"Getting material for your novel?"

"Don't be silly, I was getting relaxation and looking around. When a man is doing a lot of brain work, he has to do some playing."

"So you played around with Billy Prue?"

"Will you please let me finish?"

"Go ahead."

"Billy Prue sold me cigarettes. I looked her over and thought she was one of the most beautiful women I had ever seen."

"So you made passes?"

"Naturally. And I got absolutely nowhere."

"Then what?"

"Then I became even more seriously interested, and I'm afraid my uncle—well, I'm afraid my uncle didn't approve of the manner in which I was—doing what he called losing my head."

"What did he do?"

"I don't know, Mr. Lam. I give you my word of honor that I don't know."

"But what do *you* think?"

"I don't even think."

I said, "Perhaps I can do some thinking for you."

He looked at me with swollen, bloodshot eyes and acted as though he were a wounded deer asking me why I'd shot him.

I said, "Your uncle thought she was a gold digger?"

"I think that was rather obvious from what I said."

"So he went to see her and told her that if she'd give you a thorough jolt so it would cure you—if she'd run off with someone else, or let you catch someone else in her apartment, or do something that would completely disillusion you, he'd give her more money than she could hope to get by making a legitimate matrimonial alliance and then trying to collect alimony."

Archie took a soggy handkerchief from his hip pocket, started twisting it around and around his fingers. "I don't know," he said. "I don't know. I don't think that Uncle Rufus would have done anything like that. I don't think Billy would have listened to it. I think she would have—resented it."

"With a hand ax?" I asked.

"My God," he said, "you're driving me mad with those

cynical nasty cracks of yours. Of course not! Billy wouldn't harm a flea. We've *got* to keep Billy out of this! We must!"

"How about the picture?"

"I took it down as soon as I found out that—well, about what had happened."

"She gave you the picture?"

"No. I found out what photographer took her publicity pictures and bribed him to take a nice pin-up picture for me. She didn't know I had a print."

I said, "So far you've been one hundred percent."

"One hundred percent what?" he asked.

"Rat," I said and walked out leaving him gazing reproachfully after me, a tear-soaked handkerchief held to his nose.

Chapter Nine

A Hell of a Mess

THE APARTMENT HOUSE where I had been able to get a single apartment by dint of some pull and a lot of luck was about three blocks from the place where Bertha Cool had her apartment, which was altogether too close. It was a swanky place with a private switchboard and a garage, a rather ornate lobby, and the rent must have been fixed when the OPA had its back turned.

I parked the agency car, went up to the lobby desk, and said, "Three forty-one."

The man behind the desk looked at me sharply. "You're new here?" he asked.

I nodded. "Just checked in today."

"Oh, yes. Mr. Lam, isn't it?"

"Yes."

"There's a message for you."

He handed me my key and the folded slip of paper. The paper said: *Call Bertha Cool, at once.*

"Also," the manager went on, "a young woman has been calling you every ten or fifteen minutes. She won't leave her name or number. Says she'll call back."

"A *young* woman?" I asked.

The manager smiled condescendingly. "Her voice sounds young and attractive."

I pushed Bertha's message down in my pocket and went up to my apartment.

The telephone was ringing as I entered. I closed the door, went into the bathroom, washed my hands and face, and waited until it had quit ringing. Then I walked back to the telephone and said to the switchboard operator, "Don't call me any more tonight."

The operator said, "I'm sorry, I told this party that you didn't answer. She seemed very much disturbed, said it was a matter of the greatest importance."

"Woman?" I asked.

The girl downstairs said it was.

I changed my mind and said, "All right, go ahead and ring if the call comes in again. I'll take it."

I hadn't taken time to unpack when I'd checked in. Now I threw my grip on the bed and started taking things out. One thing about the Navy, it teaches a man to cut his possessions down to the minimum.

I yawned, turned down the bed and got out my pajamas.

The telephone rang.

I answered it.

Bertha Cool's voice said, "Well, for Christ's sake! What's the matter with you? Are you getting so damned high hat you can't call your boss on a matter of business?"

"Partner," I said.

"All right, partner then. Why the hell didn't you call me when you came in?"

"I was busy."

"Well, you're going to be busy. You're in a hell of a mess. Get over here."

"Where?"

"My apartment."

I said, "I'll see you in the morning."

Bertha said, "You'll see me now or you'll wish the hell you had. Frank Sellers is over here and the only thing that's keeping you out of the hoosegow right now is the fact that Frank is my friend. Of all the damn fools, trying to cut corners with the cops. I don't know why the hell I should worry about you. I should let you get thrown in the can. It might do you some good."

"Put Sellers on the phone," I said.

Bertha said, "You'd better come over."

"Put him on the phone."

I heard Bertha say, "He wants to talk with you."

A moment later, Sellers's voice rumbled into the telephone.

I said, "Listen, Frank, I'm all in. I don't want to go

round and round with Bertha over some trivial techni-
cality. Now suppose you tell me what's the beef."

Sellers said, "You know what the beef is, and don't
pull any of that innocent stuff with me, or I'll push your
teeth down your throat. I'm sticking my neck all the
way out to protect Bertha in the thing, and it may break
me at that."

"What the hell are you talking about?"

"You know what I'm talking about. Of all the damn,
dumb places to plant the murder weapon, that was it."

"What murder weapon?"

"The hand ax, dope."

"And where am I supposed to have planted it?" I
asked.

"Don't make me laugh," Sellers said.

"I'm kidding on the square."

"Don't be a sap," Sellers told me. "You're in so deep
now, the only way you can get out is by coming absolutely clean. If you don't do that, you're going to take a
little ride with me, and you're both going to lose your
licenses. Now then, how soon can you get over here?"

"Exactly five minutes," I said, and hung up the telephone.

Bertha's apartment was on the fifth floor. My knees
were weak as I stepped out of the elevator. I suddenly
realized I was tired. It seemed like a mile to Bertha's
door. I pushed the button.

Bertha opened the door.

The smoky aroma of good Scotch whisky tingled my
nostrils. I looked past Bertha and saw Frank Sellers sitting in his shirt sleeves, his feet elevated on a stool, a
glass in his hand. He was frowning into the glass and
looked as worried as a big cop can look.

"Well, come in," Bertha snapped at me. "Don't stand
there staring at me."

I walked in.

Bertha, in a loose-fitting house dress, said, "My God,
you've done some dangerous things in your time, but
this is the first time you've ever gone plumb dumb on

me. Of all the boob things to do. I suppose it was the legs."

"What legs?" Frank Sellers asked.

Bertha said, "When this guy gets around a girl with looks and legs, he loses all sense of perspective."

Sellers said mournfully, "*That* explains it then."

"That doesn't explain a damn thing," I told him. "You should know by this time that if you listen to her, you'll wind up behind the eight ball."

Sellers tried to grin. It was a grimace.

Bertha said, "Don't try to kid me out of it because you can't make it stick."

Sellers said, "I hate to do it to you, Donald, but you've led with your chin. You're going on the carpet, and you're probably going to lose your license. I *may* be able to keep Bertha out of it, but you're in. And you're in bad."

"Wait until you hear what he says," Bertha snapped at Sellers. "Don't go pushing your weight around on Donald."

Sellers said somewhat sullenly, "I'm not pushing any weight around, I'm telling the boy, that's all."

"Well, you don't need to tell *him*," Bertha said bristling with belligerency. "He's got more brains than you'll have if you live to be a thousand."

Sellers started to say something, then changed his mind and sipped his drink.

Bertha's eyes were suddenly solicitous. "You're white as a sheet, lover, what's the matter. You aren't letting this get you down, are you?"

I shook my head.

Bertha said, "You were supposed to take it easy. You told me that yourself. You—*have you had dinner?*"

Her question caught me by surprise. I thought back, trying to remember what I'd done with my time and then said, "No. Come to think of it, I haven't."

Bertha said, "That's just like you, coming home half sick with your system full of tropical bugs and your resistance run down, under orders to avoid excitement and take it easy, and you go stir up a murder case and then go without your dinner."

Bertha glowered at the two of us, then said, "Now, damn it, I suppose I've got to cook something for you."

"There's a place down the street," I told her, "that's still open. I'll see what the law has to say, and go down there."

"That joint!" Bertha snorted, and moved out toward the kitchen, her big body flowing along with a smooth grace inside of the loose house dress.

Sellers said, "Where did you get the hand ax, Donald?"

"Shut up," Bertha snapped, turning to glare over her shoulder at him. "You're not going to bullyrag the boy on an empty stomach. Have a drink of Scotch, lover, and come out here in the kitchen."

I took a drink and went out to the kitchen. Sellers tagged along.

Bertha broke eggs into a bowl, dumped sliced bacon into a frying-pan, shoved a pot of coffee on the stove, moving with an unhurried, ponderous efficiency that was deceptive because it didn't seem she was moving fast.

Frank Sellers sat down in the little breakfast nook and put his drink on the table in front of him. He fished a fresh cigar out of his pocket and said, "Where did you get the hand ax?"

"What hand ax?"

Bertha said, "They've found the ax in the agency car, lover. The handle had been sawed off so it was only eight and a half inches long and the sawing wasn't a neat job. It had been sawed part way through on one side, then turned around and sawed some more on the other side."

Sellers looked at my face. I met his eyes, shook my head, and said, "It's a new one on me, Frank."

"Tell him how it happened you found it, Frank," Bertha said. "I believe the little bastard's telling the truth."

Sellers said, "The police aren't so dumb, you know."

"I know."

"Well," Sellers said, "we went out to see Archie Stanberry. He was all broken up with grief, but he'd learned about the killing before we'd got there and—"

"How do you know that?" I asked.

"The way he acted," Sellers said. "He was putting on an act that he'd rehearsed. He was all suave smiles when he greeted us, and wanted to know what he could do. We asked him a few questions and he was just *too* sweet and innocent. Then we told him and he was knocked for a loop—but it was acting. You could tell that. He made the mistake most people do of putting it on just a little too thick. Nothing you could prove in court, but something you could tell, just the same."

I nodded.

"Okay," Sellers said. "We pretended to take the guy at face value, told him a few things, then went out and tapped his telephone line and put a couple of shadows on the job to see who called on him."

Again I nodded.

"You showed up in the agency car. You went inside and the boys thought it might be a good plan to give your car the once over, just to make sure about the registration certificate and all that. They didn't recognize you, and they didn't recognize the car. Remember, you've been out of circulation for a while."

Again I nodded.

"Okay," Sellers went on wearily, "they cased the back of the car and there was a nice little short-handled hand ax. They gave it a once over and there was blood on it. They handled it too damn much, but you can't blame them for that. After all, they were just a couple of leg men on a routine chore."

The aroma of bacon mingled with that of coffee. Bertha carefully poured grease off the bacon, turned it over in the frying-pan and switched on the electric toaster, dropped in a couple of pieces of bread and pulled down the control mechanism. "How did that murder weapon get in your car, Donald?"

"It *was* the murder weapon?" I asked Sellers.

He nodded.

I said, "I'm darned if I know."

"You'll have to do better than that," Sellers said.

"The little bastard's telling the truth," Bertha announced.

"How do you know?" Sellers asked.

"Because," Bertha flared at him, "if he was telling a lie, he'd have one that sounded convincing as hell, and he'd have it all ready. That business of saying, 'I don't know' is because he's either dumb or innocent, and he isn't dumb."

Sellers sighed, turned his eyes back to mine.

I said wearily, "Okay. Let's start in at the beginning. I got the agency car. I went down to the County Clerk's Office to look up some records. I fooled around the Bureau of Vital Statistics. I went out to the Rimley Rendezvous. I got kicked out and came back to the office. Then I went out to look up a witness and left the car parked there—"

"You'll have to do better than that," Sellers said. "On the witness, I mean."

"A witness that doesn't have anything to do with the murder."

"You're in a jam, Donald."

I said, "All right. This witness lived out on Graylord Avenue."

"What number?"

I said, "Nix on it. You'd rock the boat."

He shook his head and said, "It's the hammer they killed him with, Donald. I'm standing between you and the D.A.'s office right now."

I said, "Philip E. Cullingdon, 906 South Graylord Avenue."

"What's he got to do with it?"

"It's another case."

"What time did you get out there?"

"I don't know."

"How long were you there?"

I rubbed my chin and said, "I can't say, Frank. Long enough for an ax to have been planted, I guess."

"Cullingdon, eh?" Sellers said.

I nodded.

Sellers lurched up from the little bench in the breakfast nook, hitting the table and all but upsetting the drinks.

Bertha looked up from the stove and said, "Damn you, Frank Sellers, if you spill any of *that* whisky I'll brain you. That's customers' whisky."

He didn't even look at her, and went in to the telephone. I heard him turning the pages of the telephone book, then after a while heard the sound of the dial on the telephone and low-voiced conversation.

"You're in Dutch," Bertha said to me.

I didn't say anything. There was no use.

Bertha tore off a paper towel, folded it, put it on the top of a shelf over the stove, put the bacon on that to drain, poured a little thick cream into the eggs, beat them up, dumped them into the frying-pan, and started stirring.

The whisky felt warm in my stomach and I didn't feel quite as much as though someone had pulled out the plug and let all of my vitality drain out through my toes.

"You poor little bastard!" Bertha said sympathetically.

"I'm all right."

"Have another drink."

"I don't want any more, thanks."

"Food's what you need," Bertha said. "Food and rest."

Sellers hung up the telephone, then dialed another number and talked. Then he hung up the telephone and came back to the table. He'd refilled his whisky glass while he was in the sitting-room. He looked at me with puzzled scrutiny, started to say something, then checked himself and jiggled the table once more as he sat down.

Bertha glowered at him for his clumsiness, but didn't say anything.

A moment later, Bertha slid a plate over to me that had hot scrambled eggs, toast with lots of butter, golden bacon, fried just right, and a big cup of coffee with little cream gobules floating on the top. "Sugar it to suit yourself," she said. "I remember you take cream."

I dumped in sugar and nodded my thanks. The coffee turned the warmth that had been kindled in my stomach into a solid, substantial glow. The food tasted good. It was the first time I'd had a real appetite for months.

Bertha watched me eat. Sellers frowned into his drink.

"Well," Bertha said, "this is a hell of a party."

No one said anything.

"Did you get him?" Bertha asked Sellers.

He nodded.

"Well?" Bertha said.

Sellers shook his head.

"All right, clam up if you want to," Bertha snapped at him.

Bertha sat down and Sellers reached out and put his hand over hers. "You're a good egg," he said.

Bertha glared at him. "It wouldn't hurt you to say what's on your mind."

Sellers said, "Cullingdon is gun-shy. Too many people have tried to get him to talk by too many different arguments. What's more, he'd gone to bed. He was sore."

"So what?" Bertha asked.

Sellers just shook his head.

I took another sip of coffee and said to Bertha, "Be your age. He contacted a prowl car and officers are on their way out. He's waiting for a report."

Bertha looked at Sellers.

Sellers looked at me, then back at Bertha. "Bright kid," he said.

"I told you the bastard had brains," Bertha announced.

"Let's go back to your story," Sellers said to me. "You left the car out there. You didn't say how long. See anyone else out there?"

"I could have—but no one who had any chance to plant that murder weapon."

"You tell me facts, names, and places. I'll draw the

conclusions."

"Not *some* names."

"How many?"

"One."

"I want it."

"You don't get it—yet."

"You're in bad."

"Not that bad," I told him.

"I think you are."

I just kept on eating.

Bertha glared at me as though she could bite my head off. "If you don't tell him, I will," she said.

"Shut up," I told her.

Sellers looked at her expectantly.

"I'm going to," Bertha said.

"You don't even know," I pointed out.

"The hell I don't. Any time you've been spending the partnership funds to get three packages of cigarettes and then get that moony expression on your face when the sergeant asks you a simple question, I know the answer, and don't think for a damn minute that I don't. After all, in one way you can't be blamed. You've been down in the South Seas for so long you've got your head filled with a lot of romantic ideas about womanhood. You come back and the jane that you'd have called a broad a couple of years ago looks like a vision of loveliness made and handed down with a heavenly aura still clinging to her."

Sergeant Sellers looked at Bertha with admiration. "Hell, you're romantic," he said. He reached out and took her hand.

Bertha jerked her hand out from under his and said, "I'll bust you on the jaw one of these days, if you keep making passes at me."

Sellers grinned, "*That's* the way I like women—practical and hard."

Bertha simply glared at him.

I said, "Women like to think they're soft and feminine, Frank."

He looked at me in surprise.

Bertha said to me, "Keep your damn mouth shut. You've got troubles of your own."

I pushed the empty coffee cup across at Bertha and said, "Guess you'll have to do the honors."

Bertha refilled the coffee cup.

The telephone rang.

Sellers didn't even wait for Bertha to move toward it. He spilled coffee over the edge of my cup into the saucer as he made for the living-room.

Bertha called after him, said, "Just like a bull in a China shop, a big flat-foot cop trying to act civilized. Just a minute, lover, I'll fix it."

She went over to the sink and emptied the saucer, put more coffee in the cup, brought it back, and said, "Hold your hat when the big ape sits down again. He'll probably pull the damn table out by the roots this time. What's the matter? Didn't Bertha cook the bacon right?"

I nodded, said, "What I ate tasted fine."

"Well, eat the rest of it."

I shook my head.

"Why not?"

"I don't know. It's been like that lately. I'll be hungry then just a few mouthfuls of food, and my stomach turns. I couldn't get another bite down to save myself. This is the most I've eaten for a long time. I was really hungry tonight."

"Poor kid," Bertha said sympathetically, sitting down at the corner place.

I sipped the coffee. Bertha's little greedy eyes regarded me with a motherly solicitude.

After a while, Sergeant Sellers came walking back into the room. He was frowning, and so absent-minded he'd forgotten to take his drink along and pour in fresh whisky.

Bertha grabbed up my cup and saucer and held it above the table while Sellers sat down. Then she put it back on the table and said, "Well, what about it?"

Sellers said, "It's okay. A couple of guys went out in

a prowl car and shook this guy down. He says Donald
came out and asked him questions about an automobile
accident. By God, that's once you fooled me."

"How?" I asked.

"When you said it was something that didn't have
anything to do with this case. I'd have bet eight weeks
salary against a thin plugged dime that that was a run-
around. But the guy says you were asking him about an
automobile accident that took place quite a while ago.
Then he says a girl came out and claimed to be a reporter for one of the newspapers and started asking him
questions about the same accident. He rang up the newspaper she claimed to be representing and found it was
an act she was putting on, so he chased her out."

Bertha looked at me with eyes that were just a little
apprehensive.

Sellers went on: "Okay, the way I dope it out, Donald
was a little careless, but he isn't exactly a fool. He had
this man Cullingdon spotted, went out to talk with him.
The jane tagged Donald out there. Donald wasn't so
damn dumb. He knew she was tailing him. He waited
until she went in and then he pulled a fast one on her.
Cullingdon says he went to the window and looked out
to see if he could get the license number of the girl's car.
He saw her get into her car, then Donald climbed out
of his car, walked over and raised his hat to the girl.
Donald was evidently telling her off. Then he climbed in
the car and drove away with her. Cullingdon said Donald was careful to walk around the front of the car when
he went around to get in, keeping a hand on it all the
time so the girl couldn't give him the slip without a
chance to hop the running-board. Cullingdon thinks
Donald is a pretty smart egg."

"He is," Bertha said.

"So Cullingdon sort of kept an eye on things," he said.
"He admits that he went out to Donald's car and looked
at the registration to check up on Donald. Donald was
telling him the truth. He'd given him his right name and
told him what he was there for. That's a point in Don-

ald's favor."

I sipped coffee and didn't say anything.

"The car was parked out there for quite a while, Cullingdon says. He looked out every once in a while and it was still there. Then he looked out and it was gone. He didn't see Donald come and get it. Now then, if Donald can tell us—"

I opened my wallet and took out the taxicab slip that I keep for my expense-account voucher. I handed it to Sellers and said, "That's the taxicab that took me out there."

"Where did you pick it up?" Sellers asked.

"Somewhere on Seventh Street," I said casually. "I can't tell just where."

Sellers heaved a sigh and said, "Well, I guess this will do it all right. Someone planted the weapon in that car while it was parked out there in front of Cullingdon's. Now who the hell could have done that?"

I said, "That's a job for the police department. I'm going home and get some shut-eye."

Sellers said, "Your friend Cullingdon appreciates the fact that you told him the truth, Donald. And incidentally, it's a darn good thing, from the standpoint of the police department, that you did. Cullingdon said to tell you that the amount of the settlement was seventeen thousand, eight hundred and seventy-five dollars, and that the case, he thinks, was handled on a contingency basis, and her lawyers got either a third or a half."

I said, "That's nice of him."

Sellers frowned and said, "The hell of it is that you *were* investigating another matter. I can't get over that."

Bertha said, "We're a big agency. We have a lot of irons in the fire."

Sellers looked at her thoughtfully and didn't say anything.

"Well," I said, "I'm going home and get some sleep. I'm all in."

"You poor kid, you look it," Bertha said.

Sellers followed me to the door with Bertha. He said,

"After all, Lam, I should have known better. You wouldn't have done anything so dumb as to have found that weapon and then dumped it in the back of the automobile."

"Any fingerprints on it?" Bertha asked almost too casually.

"Just prints of the two guys that picked it up and looked it all over before they knew what it was," Sellers said. "Any murderer who has sense enough to toss a murder weapon into the back of somebody's automobile certainly has sense enough to wipe off the handle."

"But the head of it?" Bertha asked.

"Bloodstains and a couple of hairs that showed up under the microscope. It's the murder weapon, all right."

"Thanks for the food," I told Bertha.

Bertha's tone was maternally tender. "You're entirely welcome, lover. Now you get to sleep and get a good night's rest and don't let anything bother you. After all, we're not mixed up in this murder case and we're not going to get mixed up in it. And we've done two hundred dollars worth of work in that other matter."

"Good night," I said.

Sellers and Bertha chimed in a chorus. "Good night." Both voices were friendly.

Chapter Ten

TIGHT SQUEAK

THE THREE BLOCKS back to my apartment house seemed to be three miles. I went down into the garage and grinned at the attendant. "I'm going to have to take my car out again," I said.

He looked at the two-bits I handed him as though it were an insult rather than a tip, then moved a couple of cars and jerked his thumb toward the agency car. "There it is."

I got in, started the motor, and eased it out of the garage. I ran down the street for half a dozen blocks and pulled in to the curb and parked. I waited for about five minutes then started up, gave it the gun, went around the corner fast, and did a couple of figure eights around blocks.

No one was following me.

A fog had drifted in from the ocean and now it was beginning to settle. The air had turned cold, and the damp chill went clean through to my bones. I'd be all right for a while and then the weakness would grip me and my blood, thinned from the tropics and weakened by bugs, would turn cold, and I'd shiver and shake the way I did when the old malarial chills would get me. But these spells only lasted for a minute or two and then I'd be myself again. It was just weakness.

I drove up to the Hall of Justice, found a good place to park, and parked the bus.

I waited for half an hour that seemed like eternity. Then Billy Prue came bustling out of the lighted entrance, looked up and down the street, turned to the right, and started walking with quick, businesslike steps as though she knew exactly where she was going.

I waited until she had nearly a block head start, then slipped the car into gear.

After a couple of blocks she began to look around for a taxicab.

I slid the car up close to the curb, rolled down the window, and said, "Want a lift?"

She looked at me at first dubiously, then with recognition, then with anger.

"You may as well," I said. "It doesn't cost any more."

She came across and jerked the door open. "So *you* snitched on me. I should have known it."

I said wearily, "Don't be a damn fool. I'm trying to give you a break."

"How did you know I was here?"

"It's a long story."

"You'd better tell it."

I said, "Somebody planted the murder weapon in my car while it was parked out in front of Cullingdon's place."

Her startled gasp of surprise might have been overdone or it might not.

I said, "Naturally, they hauled me over the coals. Bertha Cool, that's my partner, thought you'd snared me into it."

"And so blabbed to the police?"

"Don't be silly. She isn't that dumb."

"Well, how did it happen—?"

I said, "Bertha Cool was sore. She made some crack about me having bought three packages of cigarettes and Frank Sellers, of Homicide, apparently didn't even notice the crack. That's when I knew where you were."

"I don't get it," she said.

I said, "Sellers isn't so dumb. If he hadn't known all about you, he'd have jumped on that opening about the three cigarette packs and pried enough information out of Bertha so he'd have known what he was after. He ignored it—just didn't seem to hear it, so I knew he'd found out all about you. And if he'd found out all about you before he came to call on me, it was a damn good bet that you were being held at the D.A.'s office. The only thing I didn't know is whether they were going to hold you or turn you loose. I couldn't have stuck it out for more than another half-hour, but I—"

A shivering fit gripped me. I put on the brake and slowed the car, but by gripping the wheel, didn't show how I was shaking.

Billy Prue kept looking at me. After a minute the fit passed and I speeded up the car again.

"So," Billy Prue said, "I came out and you were waiting—for what?"

"To see you."

"What about?"

"To compare notes."

"On what?"

"How did that murder weapon get in my car while it was parked out at Cullingdon's?"

"I don't know."

"Try again."

"I'm telling you the truth, Donald. I don't know."

I said, "I don't like to be played for a fall guy."

"I shouldn't think you would."

"And when I don't like something, I do something about it."

"I'm telling you I don't know anything at all about it."

I drove along slowly and said, "Let's look at the thing this way. You go out to Cullingdon's. You're frightened. You want a witness. You take me back and pull a razzle-dazzle about finding Stanberry's body. Then you go to Rimley's and I duck out as you could have known I would. I walked a half a dozen blocks before I found a cab. The cab took me up to 906 South Graylord Avenue and I picked up my car and drove back to the agency, had a talk with my partner, and then drove out to see Archie Stanberry."

"Well?" she asked as I stopped.

"There was plenty of time for Rimley to have the murder weapon dropped in my car before I got there," I said.

"And you think he dashed out and planted the

weapon and—?"

"Don't be silly. He simply picked up the telephone and said to someone, 'Donald Lam's car is parked out at 906 South Graylord Avenue. It would be a swell place for the police to discover the murder weapon because Billy Prue had him with her when the body was discovered. The police will think he's mixed up in it and—'"

"Baloney!" she interrupted.

I said, "I know—it's easy to pull that stuff."

"If you'd use your head for a minute, you'd realize that that would be the last thing on earth that Pittman Rimley would do. The minute you are brought into it, that attracts attention once more to me. That's why they had me down at the D.A.'s office and gave me such a grilling. I couldn't understand it, unless it was because you had double-crossed me."

I pulled the car in to the curb and stopped. It was a quiet, business street with virtually no traffic and a few lights. The little one-story store buildings were all closed up.

"Is this where I get out and walk?" she asked nervously.

I said, "I've got something to say."

"Go on and say it."

I said, "I went out to the Rimley Rendezvous. You told me to get out. I didn't get out. The head waiter sent me in to see Rimley. Rimley told me to get out and stay out."

"Well," she said, "tell me something I didn't know already."

I said, "Rimley's wrist watch was an hour fast. The clock on his mantel was an hour fast."

She sat absolutely motionless. I don't think she was even breathing.

"Is *that* something new?" I asked.

She kept perfectly still.

I said, "We found the body of Rufus Stanberry in your bathtub. His wrist watch was an hour *slow*."

"What does Mr. Master Mind deduce from that," she asked, trying to be facetious and making a botch of it.

"From that," I said, "I deduce that Rimley was building himself an alibi. He arranged to have his clock and his watch an hour fast. Probably Stanberry had been in there. Perhaps shortly before that Stanberry went into the rest room and took off his wrist watch when he washed his hands. The rest room attendant was under orders to set the watch an hour fast."

She said without any particular expression, "An hour fast?"

"That's what I said."

"But you just said that when we found his wrist watch, it was an hour slow."

"Do I have to dot all the *i*'s and cross all the *t*'s?"

"You'd better. Since you started making *i*'s and *t*'s—you'd better finish them up artistically."

I said, "Rimley was working out a slick alibi. Stanberry went in to see Rimley after his watch had been tampered with. Rimley took occasion to call Stanberry's attention to the time. Stanberry didn't realize it was that late, but he checked his watch with Rimley's clock. And then to reassure him, Rimley showed him his wrist watch. From there on it's just a case of too many cooks spoiling the broth."

"What do you mean?"

I said, "When you discovered Stanberry's body, you knew that his watch should be an hour fast. You didn't know what time it was because *you* don't wear a wrist watch. You simply took it for granted that Stanberry's wrist watch was an hour fast, so you set it back an hour. But someone else, who also knew that the wrist watch was an hour fast, had already set it back an hour."

She was silent for so long that I looked at her to see if she might have fainted.

"Well?" I asked.

"I haven't anything to say—not to you."

I said, "Okay," and started the motor.

"Where are we going?"

"Back to Bertha Cool's apartment."

"What's at Bertha Cool's apartment?"

"Sergeant Frank Sellers of Homicide."

"And what are you going to do there?"

"Tell him what I told you and let him do the talking from then on. I've been a sucker long enough."

She stuck it out for a dozen blocks, then reached over and twisted the key in the ignition. "Okay," she said, "shut it off."

"Going to talk?"

"Yes."

I eased the car to the curb and settled back against the cushions. "Go ahead."

She said, "I'd get killed if they knew I told you this."

"You'll be arrested for first-degree murder if you don't."

"You're hard when you want to be."

I fought against another spell of shivering as the cold, damp fog penetrated into the marrow of my bones, and managed to say threateningly, "I'm as hard and as cold as the back of a barred jail door."

She said in a tone of resignation, "All right, what do you want to know?"

"Everything."

She said, "I can't tell you everything, Donald. I can tell you the things that concern me. I can tell you enough so that you'll realize you're not being framed. But I can't tell you the things that relate to others."

I said, "You tell me the whole story here and now and without waiting for reinforcements or you get a third degree from Sergeant Frank Sellers. Make up your mind."

She said, "That isn't fair."

"It's fair to me."

"It's not fair to put me in that position."

"Make up your mind. I've stuck my neck out for you a couple of times. Now I'm getting tired of it. You can start paying me back, beginning right now."

She said, "I could get out of this car and start walking away. You wouldn't dare try to wrestle me back into it."

"Try it and see what happens."

I was shivering again now, but she was so intent on her own predicament that she didn't realize it.

She sat silently for about ten seconds, then she said, "How did you think Rufus Stanberry made his money?"

I said, "You're doing the talking."

"Blackmail."

"Keep talking."

"We didn't know it for quite a while."

"Who's we?"

"Pittman Rimley."

"What happened when he found out?"

"He got busy."

"Tell me about the blackmail."

"It wasn't just the usual thing. He was clever as the very devil. He did lots of embellishment and embroidery —the little things that really got in the big money."

"Mrs. Crail, for instance?"

"Exactly. He didn't bother with her on the small stuff, but waited until she got married and then cashed in in a big way—and he was doing it so that there wouldn't really have been any comeback. He was selling her the building at a price about three times what it was worth."

"Nice business if you can get it," I said.

"He was getting it. He did it in such a way there was almost no comeback. Most of the time his victims didn't even know him personally. He *may* have been blackmailing people he didn't know by sight."

"How come?"

"He has some sort of an organization, of course—a little secret service that gets the goods. But Stanberry's cleverness was in the way he'd save information for months or years—until the time was ripe for a good killing. Then the victim would get a telephone call—just one."

"What would be said?"

"A nice little threat and orders to pay money in cash to his dear nephew, Archie. After that there might be an anonymous letter or two, but usually that first telephone call was so devastating the rest was just a mop-up that Archie could handle."

I said, "Archie's eyes were all swollen with tearful grief—induced by breaking open a cigarette and putting a little grain of tobacco in each eye. I had to help him get one out. I saw the broken cigarette on his dresser."

She didn't say anything.

I said, "Archie had had your picture on his wall."

"He'd taken it down, hadn't he?" she asked quickly.

"Yes. He said it was a pin-up picture he'd bribed your publicity photographer—"

"Blackmailed was the word he should have used," she said bitterly. "Archie's a poor sap. His uncle had brains —dangerous brains."

"And where did Rimley come in? Don't make me laugh by telling me he was blackmailing Rimley."

"He was, in a way. But, of course, it was indirect."

"How?"

"Blackmailing Rimley's clients, using the Rendezvous to pick up stuff that he could use later. But he was able to keep under cover and do a lot of his stuff before we found out what was happening. It was the Crail deal that really put us wise. And, of course, Rimley had quite a stake in that. His lease lapsed within ninety days after a bona fide sale."

"So Mrs. Crail really didn't want to buy, and Rimley really didn't want to have Stanberry sell. Is that it?"

"Something like that."

"What's the rest of the deal?"

"I don't know. All I know is that Stanberry had a whole safe full of papers and we got them."

"Who did the getting?" I asked.

She said simply, "I did."

I jerked up in my seat with the sheer surprise of that. *"You* got them!"

"Yes."

"When?"

"This afternoon."

"How?"

She said, "It worked out just about as you figured. You know the washrooms there at the Rendezvous, they have a colored grafter who turns on water in the bowl, sprinkles in a little toilet water, hands you some soap and a towel and stands poised solicitously with a brush, all ready to go to work as soon as your hands are dried, which, of course, means a nice tip. Stanberry always washed his hands as though he wanted to make the scrubbing last until Saturday night. He'd take off his wrist watch and hand it to the attendant. Rimley simply instructed the attendant to set the watch ahead an hour."

"Then what?"

"Then, almost as soon as Stanberry went back to the dining-room, Rimley sent for him. And, of course, Rimley had fixed the watch and the clock in his own office."

"All right," I said, "that accounts for that much of it. Now tell me how he happened to be in your apartment."

"Don't you get the sketch?"

"No."

"He was blackmailing *me*."

"Over what?"

She laughed and said, "Over some bait that I gave him. When Rimley wanted to stop his blackmailing activities, he needed a decoy. I was it."

"And so?"

"Archie Stanberry had been making little passes at me. I let Archie get the bait and take it to his uncle. The uncle swallowed it."

"What did he find out about you?"

She smiled. "I was wanted for murder."

"Any foundation?"

"Of course not. It was a plant. I had some old newspaper clippings and a couple of incriminating letters that I'd written to myself and a few other things in a drawer in the table where Archie could find them. He found them, read them, and took them to uncle."

"And what did uncle do?"

"Called on me this afternoon, you dope. Haven't you got the play yet?"

"And you cracked him over the head with a hatchet?"

"Don't be silly. I slipped him a drugged drink that was due to make him unconscious for just about an hour and fifteen minutes."

I said, "I get it now. You had an appointment with him for a definite time. You made some mention of the time when he came in so that he would see that he was exactly on time. Then when he became unconscious you'd set his watch *back* to the right time, tell him that he'd only been out for ten or fifteen minutes; that it must have been a spell with his heart, and let it go at that."

"Exactly."

"And during that hour and fifteen minutes, what were you doing?"

"During about forty-five minutes of that time, I was playing burglar."

"Did you leave any back trail?"

"I don't think so."

"How did you work it?"

She said, "About a month ago, I got an apartment in the Fulrose Apartments. I was very careful never to go there except when I knew Stanberry was out. And even then, I only stayed there overnight once in a while so the maids would find the bed had been slept in. My story was that I was a newspaper woman who was working on a story and commuting between here and San Francisco. When I get ready to give up the apartment, it's going to be because I find that I'm in San Francisco so much of the time it will be cheaper to stay at a hotel whenever I happen to be back here."

"Go on with the rest of it."

"That's just about all there was to it. He had his drugged drink, got groggy, and started for the bathroom. Then he got sleepy and half fell in the bathtub. I slipped the keys out of his pocket. We already knew that the combination of the safe was written in his notebook so it would look like a telephone number. Rufus Stanberry never trusted anything entirely to memory.

"It was duck soup. I simply whizzed out to the Fulrose Apartments, went up to my apartment, then down the hall to his, opened the door with his key, spun the combination on the safe, and cleaned it out of everything that was at all incriminating to anyone. We put Rufus Stanberry out of the blackmail business in one clean sweep."

"Then what happened?"

"You know. I got back to my apartment. He was dead."

"What did you do with the keys?"

She said, "I put them back in his pockets."

"Then what?"

She said, "I telephoned Rimley. He told me over the telephone to beat it out right away to Philip Cullingdon's place and find out everything he knew about an Irma Begley who had shaken him down in an automobile accident."

"Did you ask him why?"

"Yes."

"What did he say?"

"That Irma Begley was Mrs. Crail."

"Who told you about the amount of the settlement and about those other actions?"

"Rimley did."

"Over the telephone?"

"Yes."

"And what did he tell you to do after that?"

"He said to get out and get the stuff on Mrs. Crail, then I was to pick up some witness, very casually, make it seem accidental if possible, and go to my apartment and discover the body."

"So you picked me as a witness?"

"After you horned in on my play I thought that you might make a swell witness. The trouble was you were too good. You figured things out because of that key."

"Why the sudden interest in Mrs. Crail?" I asked.

"Because Mrs. Crail was with him in the Rendezvous. She went out when he did. And when Stanberry's car pulled away, Mrs. Crail was following it."

"How do you know?"

"Rimley told me."

"How did he know?"

"I don't know."

"And you think Rimley thought Mrs. Crail was implicated in the murder?"

"I think he thought it would be a good thing to have enough evidence— Oh, Donald, I don't know *what* Rimley thought. He's a deep one."

"All right, let's get back to the murder. You drugged Stanberry's drink. Where did you get the drug?"

"Rimley gave it to me."

"Had you ever drugged a drink before?"

"No."

"Now then, when you went out leaving Stanberry in your apartment, exactly what did you do? You locked your door, of course?"

"No, I didn't."

"Why not?"

"I was instructed not to."

"By whom?"

"Rimley."

"What was the idea?"

She said, "I was to leave a note in Stanberry's hand where he'd be sure to see it when he woke up, saying: *You've had a spell with your heart. I'm dashing down to the drugstore to get some medicine.* In that way in case Stanberry recovered consciousness before I returned, I could account for my absence."

"That's all right, but why did you leave the door of the apartment unlocked?"

"Unlocked and slightly ajar so that Stanberry would think I'd dashed out in a hurry."

"Whose idea was that?"

"Rimley's."

"I don't like it."

"Why not?"

I said, "If your story is true, it looks as though Rimley

had played you all the way through for a fall guy. It's all just too convenient—a perfect setting for murder. The man passes out in your apartment. You are instructed to leave the door open. You're sent out on an errand that— No, wait a minute!"

"What is it, Donald?"

I said, "Rimley's too smart for that. If he had wanted to frame you, he wouldn't have hit the man over the head with a hand ax. He could have put a pillow over his head and smothered him, and then it would have appeared that the drug had affected his heart. No, that tapping him over the head with a hatchet is just too crude. And it doesn't fit in with Rimley's scheme. Now I see Rimley's interest in Mrs. Crail. The note was still in Stanberry's hand when you returned?"

"Yes."

"What did you do with it?"

"Destroyed it."

I said, "Well, so far it checks. It was a nice scheme. Stanberry would have kept his appointment with you. Naturally it would never have occurred to him that his watch had been set ahead an hour and then turned back an hour. He might well have been suspicious that the drink was drugged, but would hardly have thought you'd have had time to get his keys and—his keys were important?"

"I'll say they were important. He had a lock on his door that no passkey would open. There was a very fine lock on the inner steel door of his safe and another lock on the steel door of the compartment where the incriminating papers were kept."

I said musingly, "It could have worked out just that way. On the other hand, it *could* have been a perfect setup for the murder only—"

She flung herself on me. Her arm went around my neck. Her face pressed up close to mine.

Startled, I tried to pull away.

She crushed me to her, said in my ear, "Get hot! A prowl car just swung around the corner. We've got to be necking. If they catch you and me parked out here—"

She didn't need to say any more. I kissed her.

She mumbled, "Don't be so damned platonic."

I hugged her a little tighter.

Her full red lips half parted, clung to mine. Her body pushed itself up against mine.

I heard a car stop.

"You're not in Sunday School," Billy Prue muttered.

I warmed up to my job. A flashlight beat on my face. A hard-boiled gruff voice said, "What the hell's coming off here?"

I released Billy Prue and blinked into the flashlight.

"What the hell's the idea?" the man said. "This is a business street."

Billy Prue gave him one look, then covered her face with her hands and started to sob.

The flashlight darted around through the car. "Let's have a look at you," the cop said.

I held my face up to the beating rays of the flashlight. He took in the smeared lipstick, the rumpled hair, the necktie that was pulled to one side, said, "Okay, get the hell out of here and try an auto camp next time."

I started the car and drove away fast.

Billy Prue said, "Gosh, that was a squeak!"

"You thought that up quick," I told her.

"I had to. My God, Donald! Does it always take you that long to get going?"

I started to say something and then the chill of the fog and the emotional build-up that had come when Billy Prue started necking hit me with the force of a sledge hammer. I was shivering all over. I tried to stop the car, but before I could get it stopped I was wobbling around the street.

"Say, what the hell's the matter with you?" Billy asked.

I said, "The tropics turned my blood to water and—and you started it boiling."

I brought the car to a stop.

Billy Prue pulled me out from behind the steering-wheel. "Listen," she said, "you're going to bed. Where do you live?"

"Not my apartment," I told her. "You can't take me there."

"Why not?"

"Frank Sellers will be having it watched."

She didn't say anything, just started the car.

"Where?" I asked.

"You heard what the cop told us."

Chapter Eleven

TROPICAL FEVER

I HAD A CONFUSED IMPRESSION of white lights over a portico, a row of neat little stucco bungalows. I heard Billy Prue say, ". . . my husband . . . sick . . . back from the tropics . . . thank you. . . . Extra covers . . . yes, a double."

I was dimly conscious of water running, then I was on a bed, and a steaming hot towel quieted jumpy nerves that were causing the muscles to cramp.

Billy Prue was bending over me.

"Go to sleep."

"I've got to get my clothes off."

"Don't be silly. They're off."

I closed my eyes. Warmth enveloped me and sudden oblivion.

I wakened with sunlight streaming across the bed. The aroma of fresh coffee was in my nostrils.

I knuckled sleep out of my eyes.

The door gently opened. Billy Prue peeked into the room. Her face relaxed when she saw I was awake.

"Hello," she said, "how you feeling?"

"I think I'm feeling fine. Gosh! Did I pass out last night!"

"There wasn't anything wrong with you except you were weak and completely fagged."

"Where did you get the coffee?"

"I've been shopping. There's a store down the block."

"What time is it?"

"How the hell would I know?" she said. "I don't carry a watch. You remember you pointed that out to me yesterday night when you were trying to pin a murder on me?"

Almost instantly all of the various ramifications of the Stanberry murder came crowding back into my mind.

I said, "I've got to telephone the office."

She said, "You'll eat before you do a thing. The bathroom's all yours. Don't be too long about it because I'm cooking waffles."

She went back into the kitchen. I went into the bathroom, had the luxury of a hot bath, dressed, combed my hair with a pocket comb, and went out to the kitchen. Billy had grub cooked, and I was really hungry.

She watched me with wide, thoughtful eyes. "You're a good kid, Donald," she said.

"What have I done now?"

She smiled. "It's the way you didn't do the things you didn't do," she said, "that makes you a gentleman."

"How are we registered?" I asked.

She said nothing, simply smiled at me.

I ate quite a bit before my stomach suddenly went dead on me, right in the middle of taking a bite.

I pushed the plate back.

Billy said, "Go out there and sit in the sun. If the woman who runs the place comes over and talks with you, don't be embarrassed. We haven't any baggage and she thinks we're living in sin but she's got a boy in the Navy."

I went out and sat in the sun.

The auto camp was out of town on the rim of a valley that stretched away to where a tracery of white snow-capped mountains hung against the deep blue sky.

I settled back and relaxed.

The woman who ran the place came over and introduced herself. She had a son who was on a destroyer somewhere in the South Pacific. I told her I had been on a destroyer myself, that I might have seen her son, might have even talked with him without knowing his name. She sat down beside me in the orange-blossom-scented sunlight and we both kept quiet, each respecting the thoughts of the other. After a while Billy Prue came out and sat down beside us. Then Billy said we had to go and the woman who ran the place made some excuse to get away so she wouldn't embarrass us by letting us know that she knew we didn't have any baggage.

Billy slid in behind the wheel of the agency car and started back toward town.

"Cigarette?"

"Not while I'm driving, Donald."

"Oh, yes, I forgot."

We were almost at the Rendezvous when she suddenly asked, "How much are you going to tell your friend Sergeant Sellers about what I've told you?"

"Nothing."

She slid the car in to a place at the curb and stopped.

Soft, gentle fingers that somehow had a lot of strength in them squeezed mine. "You're a good egg, Donald," she said, "even if—"

"Even if what?" I asked as she stopped.

She opened the car door. "Even if you do talk in your sleep. Good-by, Donald."

Chapter Twelve

ACCIDENT WITH ANGLES

I DROVE THE CAR to the parking-place across from the office and went up. It was half-past twelve when I latch-keyed the door of the office. Elsie Brand was out to lunch.

I heard the sound of a creaking chair from Bertha's private office, then heavy feet on the floor and the door was jerked open.

Bertha Cool stood in the doorway looking at me with icy exasperation.

"You!" she said.

"That's right."

"Why, goddamn you!" Bertha said. "Who the hell do you think you are, and what the hell do you mean by taking a powder? Here I thought you were all in. You looked like a ghost. I slave my fingers to the bone cooking eggs and bacon for you and you start philandering—"

"Do you want to quarrel in the outer office where clients can hear us?" I asked, dropping into a chair and picking up the morning paper.

"You irritating little impudent cold-blooded ingrate. Bertha used an eight-dollar bottle of whisky to square things with that flatfoot from the police force, and you go—"

I jerked my head toward the transom. "People walking up and down the corridor can hear you, Bertha. Perhaps some possible client is standing outside—"

Bertha raised her voice. "I don't give a damn *how* many clients are standing outside. I'm going to tell you this, and you're going to listen to it. If you think you can come back here and—"

A black shadow formed on the door of the office. I pointed my finger at it.

Bertha checked herself with an effort.

Someone tried the knob of the door.

Bertha took a deep breath. "See who it is, lover."

I put down the paper, crossed the room, and opened the door.

A middle-aged man with a prominent bony nose, high forehead, and big cheek bones looked past me with gray eyes that twinkled shrewdly over the rims of half glasses and said, "Mrs. Bertha Cool?"

Bertha Cool's manner mellowed. "Yes. What can I do for you?"

The man reached in his pocket. "First, permit me to introduce myself. I am Frank L. Glimson, senior partner of the firm of Cosgate & Glimson, attorneys at law. And now, Mrs. Cool, I want you to do something for me."

He extended a paper to Bertha.

Bertha took the paper mechanically and said, "We do a lot of work for lawyers, Mr. Glimson. We rather specialize in that field. Donald, put down that newspaper. This is my partner, Mr. Glimson, Donald Lam. He's been in the Navy. Just back, and already hard at work. Now what was it you wanted? Something in these papers?"

Bertha unfolded the papers.

"Why— Why— Fry me for an oyster! Why, damn you for a—!"

Glimson held up his hand. "Just a moment, Mrs. Cool. *Just* a moment. Please let me explain."

"Explain, hell!" Bertha shouted at him. "This is a summons in the case of Mrs. Rolland B. Lidfield versus Esther Witson and Bertha Cool. What in hell do you mean?"

"Just a minute, Mrs. Cool. *Just* a minute. *Please* let me explain."

Bertha whipped through the pages of the folded legal document. "Fifty thousand dollars!" she screamed. *"Fifty —thousand—dollars!"*

"Exactly," Glimson said acidly. "And if you wish to remain hostile to me, Mrs. Cool, *it is going to cost you fifty thousand dollars."*

Bertha was, for the moment, speechless.

Glimson went on smoothly, "Mrs. Cool, I am prepared to make you a proposition, a business proposition, which is why I brought the papers here myself."

Glimson looked over at me and included me with an affable smile. "Now, Mrs. Cool," he said soothingly, "we don't really think that *you* were at all negligent. We *think* that Esther Witson is the one who was solely to blame for the accident."

He beamed at Bertha Cool.

Bertha's jaw was pushed forward like a prow of a battleship. "What's your proposition?" she said ominously.

"Now, Mrs. Cool, you're angry at me."

"You're damn right I'm angry at you," Bertha screamed.

"Mrs. Cool, I'm not going to take any unfair advantage of you. I'm a lawyer and you're not. I'm going to tell you exactly what the law is. It used to be considered that the exoneration of one tort-feasor exonerated the other. But that rule has now been changed—rather it has been clarified by our courts. The case of Ramsey versus Powers, 74 Cal. App. 621 holds that when a tort has been committed, and two or more parties are alleged by the plaintiff to have jointly committed the same—"

"What the hell do *I* care about tort-feasors?" Bertha interrupted.

"Don't you see, Mrs. Cool? All that you have to do is to help us show that it really was Miss Witson who was at fault and that's all there is to it. But there's one peculiarity of the law, Mrs. Cool, and that is that in order to take a quick deposition as a matter of right, the person whose deposition is to be taken must be a party to the action. Now I don't *say* that I made you a party to the action merely in order to take your deposition, Mrs. Cool, but I am going to tell you that I want to take your deposition right here at your office at three o'clock this afternoon. And if your testimony shows that the accident was all the fault of Esther Witson, we will ask the court to dismiss the case against you on the ground that there is no liability on your part."

And Glimson beamed at her.

Bertha said, "Suppose this client of yours—what's her name?"

"Mrs. Rolland B. Lidfield," Glimson said.

"All right. Suppose Mrs. Lidfield was the one who was at fault?"

Glimson put long bony fingertips together. "Now, Mrs. Cool, I think you must have overlooked the significance of what I said to you just now. If the accident was occasioned by the negligence of Miss Witson *then* we will move the court to dismiss the action—"

"What the hell is this, bribery or blackmail?" Bertha asked.

"My *dear* Mrs. Cool! My *dear* Mrs. Cool!"

"Don't you my dear me," Bertha said. "What the hell's the idea of this thing anyway?"

"We want your deposition, Mrs. Cool. We feel that we are entitled to have your evidence perpetuated so that when the case comes up for trial we will know *exactly* what we have to contend with. In so many of these cases, Mrs. Cool, the evidence has a habit of jumping around. You'll think you have a good case, and then when you get in court— But after all, Mrs. Cool, you are a woman of the world, and you understand these things."

"I don't understand a damn thing about it," Bertha said, "except that *I'm* not going to be dragged into it. If you can show any negligence on my part, I'll eat it!"

Glimson threw back his head and laughed. "You express it so quaintly, Mrs. Cool. But you're going to feel rather foolish explaining in court why you gave the name *Boskovitche!*"

The telephone rang. I moved over to Elsie's desk and answered it.

The voice that came over the wire was vibrant with eager excitement. "Hello, hello. Who is this?"

"Donald Lam talking."

"Oh, Mr. Lam! This is Esther Witson. You know, the Miss Witson who was in that automobile accident, and who called—"

"Yes, I know."

"I want to talk with Mrs. Cool."

"She's busy now. It might be better if she talked a little later."

"But can't she come to the telephone just long enough to—"

I said, "She's busy now. It might be better if she called a little later."

Esther Witson thought that over for a moment, then said, "Oh, you mean that she's busy in connection with —something that has to do with that case?"

"Yes."

She said, "I wonder if you could answer my questions, Mr. Lam."

"I'll try."

"Is a hatchet-faced lawyer by the name of Glimson there?"

"Yes."

"Talking with her now?"

"Yes."

"Oh, Mr. Lam, I wonder if you could get this message to Mrs. Cool. My lawyer said that Glimson is trying to make Mrs. Cool a party so he can take her deposition, and that if Mrs. Cool would agree to whatever it is that Glimson wants without committing herself as to what her testimony is going to be, it would be the best way to trap Glimson in what my lawyer says is sharp practice."

I said, "I'll see what I can do."

"I'll come over a little later and explain things in detail," she said.

"I'll let you talk with Bertha," I said, and motioned to Bertha.

"I'll take it later," Bertha said.

"Better *listen* to this, Bertha. You can make up your

mind later, but *listen* now."

Bertha moved over to the phone, said, "Hello," then listened. After a while she said, "All right. Good-by," and hung up.

She turned to Glimson. "Where do you want to take this deposition?"

He beamed at her. "We can take it right here, Mrs. Cool. I'll have a notary who is also a shorthand court reporter move right in. It won't inconvenience you at all, only a few minutes—a few simple questions—"

"What time?"

"I had suggested three o'clock, but—"

"All right," Bertha snapped. "Make it three o'clock, and get the hell out of here so I can work."

Glimson's hand shot out. He shook my hand. He shook Bertha Cool's hand. He nodded his head and backed out of the office still nodding.

"The dirty damned shyster," Bertha said when the door closed on him.

I said, "Wait until after three o'clock this afternoon before you say anything. And you might start thinking over what you're going to say. I think he may be an automobile lawyer."

Bertha glowered at me. "Any time that bony-faced bastard thinks he can rattle me, he's got another think coming. Automobile lawyer my foot! I'll show *him* a thing or two."

"It's okay by me," I said, and picked up the paper again.

Bertha glowered at me and was just starting to say something when Elsie Brand fitted her latchkey to the door, opened it, and then seemed surprised as she saw Bertha and me there.

"Oh, hello! I'm not interrupting, am I?"

Bertha said angrily, "Damn it, do we always *have* to hold our conferences here in the outer office? What the hell do we have a private office for?"

Elsie Brand said, "Sorry," in an impersonal tone of voice and crossed over to her typewriter.

Bertha turned to me. "We got interrupted," she said, sudden anger in her eyes. "Where the hell did you sleep last night? Frank Sellers said you—"

She broke off as the outer door opened.

The man who entered was a broad-shouldered competent individual who at the moment looked as awkwardy self-conscious as a man at the ribbon counter of a department store. "Mrs. Cool?" he asked.

Bertha nodded.

"Mr. Lam?"

I got to my feet.

"My name," he said, "is Ellery Crail."

Bertha flashed me a glance, said hastily, "Come in. We were just on the point of going out—that's how you happened to catch us in the outer office. But we'll postpone it."

"I'm sorry to interfere," Crail apologized, "but I'm exceedingly busy and—"

"Come in," Bertha said, "come right in."

We filed into the private office. Bertha seated herself behind the desk, indicated a chair for me on her right, seated Crail in the big comfortable clients' chair.

Crail cleared his throat. "In a way," he said, "I'm not consulting you in your professional capacity."

"No?" Bertha asked, her personality withdrawing itself behind a hard shell of incipient hostility. "Then what do you want?"

Crail said, "You were, I believe, a witness to an automobile accident yesterday."

"Oh, *that!*" Bertha said.

"For reasons of my own," Crail went on, "I would like very much to have that case settled out of court, have the matter compromised and dropped."

Bertha pricked up her ears. Shrewd calculation glittered in her eyes. "Just how," she asked, "did you propose to go about it?"

Crail said, "I don't want to approach the attorneys on either side, but it occurred to me that you, being a professional woman, might be in a position to arrange for a cash settlement so that the entire matter would be dropped."

"May I ask what's your interest in it?" I inquired.

Crail said, "That's a question I'd prefer not to answer."

I said, "One of the parties to the accident wrote down the license numbers of the cars that were near by."

Crail changed position in the big chair. "Then you know the answer."

"What," Bertha demanded, "would be in it for me—for us?"

"I could," Crail said, "arrange to give you five hundred dollars if you could settle the matter for twenty-five hundred. That would make a total expenditure on my part of three thousand dollars."

"In other words," Bertha said eagerly, "you'll pay three thousand dollars to settle the case, and anything we can get between the amount of the settlement and three thousand dollars will—"

"I didn't say that," Crail interrupted with dignity. "I said that I would be willing to pay you five hundred dollars to effect a settlement up to an amount of twenty-five hundred dollars."

"Suppose we get a settlement for two thousand dollars?"

"Your fee would be five hundred."

"The same as if we settled for twenty-five hundred?"

"Yes."

"That doesn't give us very much of an incentive to get a lower settlement."

"Exactly," Crail said. "I am making my proposition in the manner in which I have outlined it for a very definite reason. I don't want you to try and increase your own compensation at the expense of delaying a settlement. I want this thing cleaned up *at once*."

Bertha said, "Now let's get this straight. All that you want us to do is settle this lawsuit over the automobile accident? That's absolutely everything?"

"That's all, yes. What else would there be?"

"I'm just getting it straight," Bertha said, "so that it won't interfere with any other work that we might have here in the office."

"I see no reason why it should, Mrs. Cool. My proposition is very simple."

Bertha said, "We'd want a retainer. At least a couple of hundred in advance."

Crail reached in his pocket for his checkbook, unscrewed the cap of his fountain pen, then thought better of it, put the cap back on the pen, the pen back in his pocket, folded the checkbook, drew out a wallet and counted out two hundred dollars in tens and twenties.

Bertha scribbled a receipt which Crail folded and tucked into his wallet. Then he got to his feet smiling inclusively. He shook hands with Bertha and me and went out.

Bertha's eyes glittered up into mine. "Well, lover, it's working out all right. Two hundred bucks here and two hundred bucks there, and the first thing you know, we'll have a real case out of it."

I said, "Why do you suppose he wants the case settled, Bertha?"

Bertha's eyebrows came up. "Why, for the simple reason that he doesn't want anyone to know his wife was following Stanberry."

I said, "Somehow, in Mrs. Crail's position, I'd hardly confide in a husband."

"Well, what you'd do, and what she's done, are two different things."

"Perhaps, but I'm beginning to wonder if this case doesn't have another angle we haven't considered."

Bertha said irritably, "That's the devil of it with you, Donald. You keep arguing against established facts. Now you're going out with Bertha and get a nice lunch so that you won't get all run down like you were yesterday night."

"I had a late breakfast," I said.

"The hell you did! Say, where were you last night? I—"

The telephone made sound. Bertha glared at me for a minute, then snatched up the receiver.

I heard Elsie Brand's voice saying, "Esther Witson is here."

"Oh, my God!" Bertha said. "I forgot she was coming. Send her in."

Bertha slammed back the receiver and said to me. "Now if we could get two hundred dollars out of *her,* we'd really be getting somewhere."

Chapter Thirteen
LEGAL MONKEY BUSINESS

ESTHER WITSON CAME BARGING IN, her face filled with toothful smiles. A couple of steps behind her, a pudgy man about two-thirds bald beamed amiably at us behind horned-rimmed glasses. He had bluish-green eyes, an appearance of beefy solidarity and a manner which was consciously dynamic. It was as though he'd been reading books on how to impress people and had remembered just about all he had read. A short red mustache, ragged and stiff as a bottle brush, separated his nose from a thick upper lip. His thick fingers clutched the handle of a briefcase.

"My lawyer, Mr. Mysgart, John Carver Mysgart. He's handled my legal interests for years," Esther Witson said.

Mysgart bowed so that the light from Bertha's window reflected from the shiny expanse of his bald dome.

"This is Mrs. Cool," Esther Witson went on, "and this is Mr. Lam."

Mysgart shook hands. He was, he announced, very pleased to meet us both.

"Won't you be seated?" Bertha asked.

Esther Witson said, "They've served papers on me. I brought my lawyer along because I wanted him to explain the legal aspects of the situation."

She turned to Mysgart and beamed at him.

Mysgart cleared his throat. The amiable expression instantly left his face as he marshaled his features into the judicial. He said, in tones of deep solemnity, "This is a legal outrage, Mrs. Cool. It is unfortunate that the legal profession is besmirched by such a firm as Cosgate & Glimson."

"Shysters?" Bertha asked.

"Not exactly what you'd call shysters," Mysgart said. "They are shrewd, aggressive, able, and scrupulous in observing the exact letter of the law. But that is all. Yes, Mrs. Cool, that is all. Understand, I wouldn't want to be quoted in this. It is merely a confidential statement that I'm making—a privileged communication, by the way."

"He's had dealings with them before," Esther Witson interposed.

Mysgart lifted his briefcase, opened it. "Take, for instance, this despicable, this damnable attempt to influence your testimony, Mrs. Cool. It is legal in the sense that there's no law against it, but it is something which the ethical lawyer can never condone. You see what they have done, don't you?"

"They've sued me," Bertha said.

"Exactly. They've named you as a defendant in order to worry you, in order to harass you, in order to annoy you, and in order to stampede you so that in giving your testimony you will be swayed by a desire to placate them."

Bertha said, "They can't scare me."

Esther Witson nodded enthusiastically, "That's exactly what I told Mr. Mysgart."

Mysgart beamed at Bertha. "I'm glad to hear you say so, Mrs. Cool. Now my idea is to turn their despicable little trick against them. You are entitled to five days notice before they can take your deposition, but these lawyers naturally didn't tell you that. They wanted to force you to testify in their favor, to intimidate you, to browbeat you. However, we've worked out a perfect defense to their little scheme, Mrs. Cool. My client was not only blameless, throughout, but she is a generous, warm-hearted, sympathetic woman who has a keen appreciation for the inconvenience to which you have been subjected.

"Mrs. Cool, my client, Esther Witson, has told me that she will defray the expenses of making a legal appearance for you. In other words, I am instructed by my client to file an answer on your behalf and proceed as your attorney until the matter is disposed of and it will

not cost you one red cent—not one red cent, Mrs. Cool.
My client will defray the entire cost of the action."

Bertha beamed all over her face. "You mean I won't
have to hire any lawyer?"

"No, Mr. Mysgart will appear for you. He'll take care
of everything," Esther Witson said.

"And it won't cost me a cent?"

"Not a red cent," Mysgart repeated.

Bertha heaved a sigh of relief and reached for a cigarette.

There was a moment's silence while Bertha lit up. I
could see Bertha struggling for a diplomatic approach.
Abruptly she blurted, "How about settling the case?"

"Settling it!" Mysgart said, mouthing the words as
though forcing himself to say something utterly repre-
hensible. "My *dear* Mrs. Cool, there is nothing to settle
—absolutely nothing."

Bertha coughed a couple of times, looked over to me
for help.

I didn't say anything.

Bertha said, "After all, you know, lawsuits are expensive. And it occurred to me that in order to avoid
all of the trouble of litigation—well, you know, I might
make some offer of settlement to the plaintiff's lawyer
to see if he'd wipe the whole thing off the books."

"Oh, don't do that! For Heaven's sake, don't do that,
Mrs. Cool! That would be an admission of liability on
your part. That would jeopardize the entire case. That
would be inconceivably disastrous!"

"Well," Bertha said, "I'm a busy woman. I can't take
the time—"

"Oh, but it isn't going to cost you anything," Esther
Witson interrupted. "Mr. Mysgart will represent you
at every stage of the proceedings and there won't be any
charge—none whatever."

"But there's my time," Bertha said lamely. "I thought
perhaps—well, you know, I'd offer them a thousand or
two and see what they did."

Mysgart and his client exchanged glances of incredulous amazement.

"You mean you'd offer it yourself out of your *own* pocket?"

"Why not?"

"But why should you?" Mysgart said. "Can't you understand, Mrs. Cool, the only reason on God's green earth that they have made you a party defendant to this action is so they could take your deposition and bullyrag you into distorting what had happened so that it would be in their favor. It's a very shrewd and a very desperate trick. They put you in the position of being a defendant faced with a large contingent liability, and then assure you that if your testimony is the way they think it is going to be, they will dismiss the action against you. It's very plainly an attempt to influence the witness."

Bertha looked over at me.

I lit a cigarette.

Bertha looked at Mysgart, floundered around for words, then suddenly turned on me and said, "Damn it, say something."

Mysgart elevated his eyebrows, glanced curiously over at me.

"Want me to tell you what I think?" I asked Bertha.

"Yes."

I said, "Go ahead, tell them the truth. Tell them that Miss Witson was driving along behind you; that you stopped your car because you wanted to turn left; that you motioned her to go on around you and she stopped to bawl you out, and that was the reason she didn't see Lidfield's car coming."

There was a silence that could have been put in a slicing machine, cut off into small slices, and wrapped up in paper.

Esther Witson said suddenly, "Well, if *that's* the position you're going to take, I'll do a little talking myself."

Mysgart said soothingly, "Come, come now, ladies. Let's—"

"Shut up," Esther Witson said. "As a matter of fact,

this fat slob was driving all over the road. First she was on the left. Then she swung way over to the right, just in front of me. Then damned if she didn't stop and start giving left-hand turn signals and then waving her arms and going through a lot of outdoor calis-thenics—"

"Who's a fat slob?" Bertha yelled.

"You are!"

"Ladies, ladies," Mysgart interposed.

"My God," Bertha said, "no horse-toothed bitch is going to call me a fat slob. I'm heavy—but I'm hard. There's nothing slobby about me. Get the hell out of here!"

"And," Esther Witson went on, "because I didn't know what you were going to do, and was trying to get past you, I was lured out into the intersection and—"

"My *dear* young lady," Mysgart said, on his feet now and between her and Bertha Cool, "you mustn't, you simply *mustn't* make such statements."

"I don't care," Esther Witson screamed. "It was all *her* fault, and as far as I'm concerned, she's the one that's responsible for the whole business."

Bertha Cool said, "You were so damned anxious to bawl me out that you damn near twisted your neck off. You weren't even looking where you were going. All I saw was those horse teeth of yours—"

"Don't you say anything about my teeth, you fat swill barrel!"

Mysgart got the door open into the corridor. "Please, Miss Witson, please—I beg of you."

Esther Witson yelled back over his shoulder. "I didn't want you for a witness, anyway. I hate fat stupidity."

"Keep your lips over your teeth as much as you can, dearie," Bertha said. "You look like hell when your mouth is *all* the way open."

The door slammed.

Bertha, her face almost purple, looked at me. "Damn you," she said, "you did that. Sometimes I could rip you apart just to see what makes you tick—only you don't tick. You're too smooth. You're just a lot of damn wheels running in an oil bath. God, how I hate you!"

I said, "Your cigarette's burning the desk."

Bertha snatched up the cigarette end, ground it out in the ash try, and glowered at me.

I said, "It had to come out sooner or later. It's better this way. You try juggling the truth and you'll get hurt. Eventually we'll settle this case for Crail, but not by letting Mysgart think he's going to have a case he can win. Esther Witson has money. If *you* settle the case, Mysgart can't charge his client a fat fee. If you're on his side, he'll put in a lot of time on legal monkey business and when he's won the case send his client a bill for about three thousand bucks. Tell the truth and Mysgart may be willing to work out a settlement. Well, I've got some work to do. See you around deposition time. Better think over what you're going to say."

I walked out of the office. Bertha, frowning at her desk, was too busy thinking to say anything.

Elsie Brand was pounding away at the keyboard of the typewriter. Without missing a beat of a single letter, she glanced up at me, her right eye slowly closed.

I winked back at her and went out.

Chapter Fourteen

BERTHA SWEATS BLOOD

IT WAS PRECISELY THREE-SEVENTEEN when I returned to the office.

The deposition was under way. A court reporter sat at Elsie Brand's desk, taking down everything that was said in shorthand. Bertha Cool was on the witness chair looking rather triumphant. The man of about fifty with a weak chin and eager greedy eyes who sat next to Frank Glimson would be Rolland B. Lidfield, one of the plaintiffs in the case.

As far as possible, John Carver Mysgart had interposed his bulk between Esther Witson and Bertha Cool. He had Esther parked pretty well behind him and he was scribbling furiously on a notebook as I opened the door, evidently taking down something he wanted to ask Bertha when it came his turn.

They all glanced up as I entered. Then Glimson went on with his questioning. His hands were out in front of his chest, the fingers spread apart, tips touching. His head was tilted back slightly and his bony face was a complete mask. "Now, Mrs. Cool, tell us exactly what *you* did."

"I slowed my car at the intersection," Bertha said, "and then I heard this raucous horn blowing behind me."

"Yes, yes, go on."

"And then Miss Witson swung her car around me out into the middle lane of traffic."

"And what did she do, if anything?"

"She started giving me a tongue lashing because she didn't like the way I was driving."

"She stopped her car to do this?" Glimson asked.

"She did not. She was shooting around me with a heavy foot on the throttle."

"She was, of course, facing you," Glimson said as one who makes a statement rather than asks a question.

"I'll say she was facing me," Bertha said.

"You saw her eyes?"

"I saw her eyes *and her teeth*."

Esther Witson moved in her chair.

Mysgart reached back and made little pattie-cake gestures with his hand to quiet down his client.

Glimson's eyes held a flashing glint of triumph. "Then when Miss Witson drove past you, she was looking at you and talking to you. Is that right?"

"That's right."

"Let me see if I have understood your testimony correctly, Mrs. Cool. I believe you said that when you came to the *intersection* you brought your car almost to a stop."

"That's right."

"Now let's not misunderstand each other. When Miss Witson went *past* you, she was looking at you and talking to you, and your car was at the intersection, is that right?"

"Yes."

"Then the front of *her* car must have been well into the intersection?"

"Well, yes."

"While she was looking at you and talking to you?"

"Yes."

"And all of this time she was traveling at a high rate of speed?"

"She was stepping on it. She had a heavy foot on the throttle."

"And when did she turn around to look where she was going?" Glimson asked.

"Well, all of a sudden, it seemed to hit her that she hadn't been looking—"

"Note an objection," Mysgart said, "that the witness cannot testify as to what seemed to have been passing through my client's mind. She can only testify—"

"Yes, yes," Glimson interrupted. "Just tell us the facts,

Mrs. Cool, not what you think."

"Or what she thinks my client thought," Mysgart added sarcastically.

Glimson glared at him.

Mysgart wiggled his upper lip so that his mustache scratched his nose.

"Well, she suddenly turned around and there was this other car right on top of her," Bertha snapped.

"You mean the car which was being driven by Mr. Rolland B. Lidfield, the gentleman sitting at my right?"

"Yes."

"And this car driven by Mr. Lidfield was turning to the left, was it not, so that it was headed up Mantica Street in a northerly direction?"

"That's right."

"And Miss Witson, with what you have described as a heavy foot on the throttle, charged her car blindly into the intersection of Garden Vista Boulevard and Mantica Street directly in front of the car driven by Mr. Lidfield. Is that right?"

"That's right."

Glimson settled back in his chair and lowered his hands until they rested across his stomach. He turned to Mysgart with a benign expression, "Would you care to cross-examine?"

Esther Witson stirred uneasily in her chair.

Mysgart made another little blind patting gesture in her general direction and said, "Certainly."

"Go ahead."

"Thank you," Mysgart retorted with heavy sarcasm.

Mysgart shifted the position of his chair somewhat. Bertha Cool glanced at me with a triumphant expression as much as to say that no damn lawyer was going to mix her up, and then turned her eager little eyes on Mysgart.

Mysgart cleared his throat. "Now let's just go back to the beginning and see if we get this straight, Mrs. Cool. You were proceeding in a westerly direction on Garden Vista Boulevard?"

"Yes."

"And how long had you been driving westerly along Garden Vista Boulevard before you came to the intersection of Mantica Street?"

"Eight or ten blocks, perhaps."

"Now at the intersection of Mantica Street, you have testified that your automobile was in the extreme right-hand lane, the lane that is next to the curb."

"Yes."

"And how long had it been in *that* lane?"

"I don't know."

"You wouldn't say for eight or ten blocks?"

"No."

"Some of the time you had been over on the extreme left-hand lane, the one that's closest to the center of the road, hadn't you, Mrs. Cool?"

"I suppose so."

"And part of the time you had been in the middle lane?"

"No."

Mysgart raised his eyebrows in surprise. "You're certain of that, Mrs. Cool?"

"Absolutely *certain*," Bertha snapped.

"At no time at all had you operated your car in the middle lane? Is that right?"

"That's right."

"But you *had* been over on the left-hand lane?"

"Yes."

"And at the time of the accident you were over on the right-hand lane?"

"Yes."

"Then," Mysgart said with elaborate sarcasm, "will you be so kind as to tell us, Mrs. Cool, how you could possibly have got from the left-hand lane to the right-hand lane without driving over the middle lane?"

"I may have *crossed* it," Bertha said.

"Oh," Mysgart said with well-simulated surprise, "then you *did* operate your car on the middle lane?"

"I went across it."

"Straight across?"

"Yes."

"Then am I to understand you turned sharply and crossed the middle lane at a right angle?"

"Don't be silly, I *angled* over to the right-hand lane."

"Oh, then you turned abruptly in front of oncoming traffic?"

"Certainly not," Bertha said. "You can't mix *me* up. I eased my way over."

"Taking perhaps a block in order to complete your maneuver, or two blocks, or three blocks, or four blocks?"

"I don't know."

"It *might* have been four blocks?"

"I don't know. . . . It could have been."

"Then for a long distance, Mrs. Cool, perhaps for as much as four blocks, you *were* operating your car in the middle lane of traffic?"

"I was easing my way across it."

"Then what did you mean by telling us that at no time did you operate your car on the middle lane of traffic?"

"Well, I meant that I wasn't—well, I wasn't going down the middle lane and intending to keep on it."

"But you did operate your car across the middle lane?"

"Across, yes."

"Then for a certain period of time you did have your car moving along Garden Vista Boulevard so that all four of its wheels were within the white lines of the middle lane?"

"I guess so, yes."

"I don't want any guessing about it," Mysgart announced. "I want the facts. Come, Mrs. Cool, if you're as expert an automobile driver as you claimed, you certainly should be able to tell us frankly and without equivocation whether you did or did not at any time within those eight or ten blocks operate your automobile so that all four wheels were within the white lines of the middle lane of the highway."

"I did, yes!" Bertha shouted at him.

Mysgart settled back in his chair with sad resignation. "Then you were testifying incorrectly, Mrs. Cool, when you said that at no time did you operate your car on the middle lane."

Bertha started to say something but the words sputtered into angry, inarticulate sounds. The court reporter looked up.

"Come, come," Mysgart said, "try and answer that question."

Bertha said, "I've told you what happened."

"Exactly. You have told me two different things, Mrs. Cool. I'm really trying to find out which is correct."

Little beads of perspiration appeared on Bertha's forehead. She said, "All right, have it your own way."

"No, no, not my way," Mysgart interposed hastily, "*your* way, Mrs. Cool. And may I caution you that you're under oath, so this time try and tell the truth."

"All right," Bertha screamed at him, "I was on the left-hand lane. I crossed over the middle lane to the right-hand lane. Now what's wrong with that?"

"A great deal *might* have been wrong with it," Mysgart said condescendingly. "It depends on how you did it. Did you give any signal before you cut across to the right-hand lane?"

"No, I didn't."

"Did you look behind?"

"Of course I looked behind."

"Turned your head?"

"No. I glanced in the rear-view mirror."

"And, because of the angle at which your car was being operated, you couldn't see the road down that lane. In other words, since you had turned your car sharply to the right, your rear-view mirror only showed the vehicles directly behind you. What I am getting at," Mysgart said soothingly, "is that you didn't see the car operated by Esther Witson which was coming behind you?"

"No, I didn't," Bertha admitted.

"When did you first see it?"

"When I got over to the right-hand curb and stopped. Then I looked up in the rear-view mirror and saw her right behind me."

"Oh, you *stopped?*"

"Yes, I stopped," Bertha said angrily. "Now try and twist something out of that."

"Did you give a stop signal when you stopped?"

"Yes, I did."

"How?"

"I put my arm out of the window on an angle."

"Your whole arm?"

"My whole arm."

"And gave a stopping signal?"

"A stopping signal," Bertha asserted.

"Now why did you stop, Mrs. Cool? You didn't have any passengers to let out at the curb, did you?"

"No."

"And you knew that this wasn't a parking-place?"

"Of course."

"You were right at the intersection?"

"Right at the intersection."

"And there was a traffic signal on Mantica Street?"

"Yes."

"And that signal was in a position that held traffic open for travel along Garden Vista Boulevard?"

"That's right."

"And yet you stopped?"

"Well, I just about stopped."

"Not whether you just about stopped, Mrs. Cool. I want to know whether you stopped."

"Well, I—I may have been moving very slowly."

"But a moment ago, Mrs. Cool, you said you stopped."

"All right," Bertha shouted at him, "I stopped, then."

"Brought your car to a dead stop?"

"To a dead stop, if you want it that way."

"Not the way I want it, Mrs. Cool, but what did you actually do?"

"All right, I stopped my car."

"To a dead stop?"

"I didn't get out and stick up my finger and sight along the edge of it to see if the car was moving," Bertha said sarcastically.

"Oh, I see," Mysgart said as though that explained everything. "I think you misunderstood me, Mrs. Cool, or I misunderstood you. As I get your testimony now, you aren't absolutely certain whether your car was at a *dead* stop or whether it was moving?"

"That's right."

"But you did give a full arm signal that you were going to stop?"

"That's right."

"A *stop* signal?"

"That's what I said."

"And that's what you meant?"

"Of course that's what I meant."

"Now let me ask you again, Mrs. Cool, why did you stop? You didn't intend to park there."

Bertha said, "I intended to turn left as soon as this other car got around me."

"Oh, you intended to turn left? Did you convey your intention by means of any signal?"

"Certainly."

"You mean you gave a left-turn signal?"

"That's right."

"And how did you do that, Mrs. Cool?"

"How does anyone do it?"

"No, no, Mrs. Cool, I want to know how *you* did it." Bertha said, "I stuck my left arm out of the window—straight out."

"A full arm signal?"

"A full arm signal."

"And then you saw this car behind you."

"Yes."

"For the first time?"

"Yes."

"And you wanted that car to go around you?"

"Yes."

"Did you convey your intention to the driver of that

car by means of any signal?"

"Certainly."

"What did you do?"

"I motioned her to go ahead."

"How?"

"By waving my arm."

"Just what do you mean, by waving your arm, Mrs. Cool?"

Bertha thrust her arm out and made a series of circular motions.

"Let the records show," Mysgart said, "that Mrs. Cool at this point extends her left arm and makes a series of circular motions—motions which go higher than her head when the arm is elevated, and down almost to the floor when the arm is lowered. That's right, Mrs. Cool?"

"That's right," she said, and then added sarcastically, "I'm glad you've got *something* right."

"And as soon as she received that signal, Miss Witson drove around you. Is that right?"

"Drove around me, giving me a piece of her mind," Bertha said.

"Now your window was down on the left-hand side, was it not?"

"Yes."

"And how about the window on Miss Witson's car?—Careful now, Mrs. Cool. I don't want to trap you. I simply want to test your powers of observation, and see what you can remember. Was the right-hand window on Miss Witson's car down or up?"

Bertha thought for a minute then said, "It was up."

"You're positive?"

"Positive."

"All of the windows on the right-hand side of Miss Witson's car were up?"

"Yes."

"All the way up?"

"That's what I said."

"And exactly what did Miss Witson say to you? What words did she use?"

A gleam of triumph came into Bertha's eyes. "You're not going to trap me that way," she said.

Mysgart raised his eyebrows. "What do you mean?"

"I mean that if the windows on the right-hand side were up, I couldn't *hear* what she was saying, and you know it as well as I do. I could *see* her talking."

"But you couldn't hear the words?"

"Naturally not. Not with the windows up."

"Couldn't hear any words?"

"No. Well, I heard— No, I won't swear to it."

"Then how do you know that Miss Witson was giving you what you have referred to as a piece of her mind?"

"I could tell it by the expression on her face."

"You didn't hear a word she said?"

"No."

"Then when you say she was giving you a piece of her mind, you're depending upon mental telepathy?"

"I could see the expression on her face."

"Can you tell what people are thinking by the expressions on their faces?"

"Yes. When their lips are moving."

Mysgart immediately moved his lips soundlessly for several seconds and then asked, "What did I say then, Mrs. Cool?"

"You didn't say anything then."

"But I was moving my lips. I was actually stating something. I made a very definite statement, Mrs. Cool. I was moving my lips, and you could see the expression on my face, couldn't you?"

Bertha didn't say anything.

"So you don't know what I said?"

Bertha took refuge in a sullen, badgered silence.

Mysgart waited for several seconds, then said, "Let the record show that the witness either cannot or will not answer the question."

Bertha was sweating now.

Mysgart went on. "So, Mrs. Cool, having suddenly shot from the left lane of traffic over to the right lane of traffic, directly in front of the car being operated by my client, Miss Witson, you suddenly gave a stop signal, slowed your car somewhat, you don't know how much because you don't know whether it was stopped or whether it was still moving. You abruptly gave a left-hand turn signal, then you suddenly gave this whole wild series of arm signals, and thereupon proceeded to block traffic completely and thoroughly so far as the right-hand lane of traffic was concerned. Can you give any logical explanation of why you did that?"

"I tell you I wanted to turn left, and I wanted this car to go around me."

"You knew that you had no right to stop in the intersection when the signal was for open traffic along Garden Vista Boulevard?"

"Well, if you want to be technical about it, yes."

"So you brought your car to an illegal stop."

"All right."

"You knew that you had no right to turn to the left from the right-hand lane of traffic?"

"Of course. That's why I wanted this other car to go by me."

"So you gave two signals for two illegal maneuvers, one right after the other?"

"Well, if you want to put it that way, yes."

"Now this car that was being driven by Mr. Lidfield, when did *you* first see it?"

"Just before the crash."

"Exactly how long before the crash?"

"I can't tell you. I'd say it was a second."

"And where was it when *you* first saw it?"

"It was just swinging into a left-hand turn."

"And you know where the actual collision took place?"

"Yes."

"Where?"

"Right in front of my car. It blocked me so I couldn't move one way or another."

"Exactly. I don't want to trap you, Mrs. Cool. I'll say that an actual survey shows that the distance from the place where the cars were found to the center of the intersection was exactly thirty-one feet. That distance seems just about right to you, does it?"

"Just about."

"It's the exact distance, Mrs. Cool. I think Counsel on the other side will agree with me."

Mysgart looked at Glimson and Glimson said nothing.

"Now then, Mrs. Cool, when you first saw this Lidfield car, it was some distance back of the intersection?"

"Well, it hadn't reached the center of the intersection yet."

"Exactly. So the car had to reach the center of the intersection, make a turn on the far side of the center of the intersection, and then go thirty-one feet before it hit the Witson car."

"I guess so, yes."

"A distance, in all, perhaps of fifty feet?"

"Well, somewhere around there, yes."

"So that you would say the Lidfield car had to travel at least fifty feet from the time you first saw it before the time of the collision?"

"I'd say so, yes."

"And you have stated positively, Mrs. Cool, that you saw the car just one second before the collision."

"That's right," Bertha said.

Mysgart said, "Has it ever occurred to you, Mrs. Cool, that a car which travels fifty feet in a second is traveling at the rate of three thousand feet a minute. And three thousand feet a minute is faster than thirty-four miles per hour?"

Bertha blinked her eyes.

"So then," Mysgart said, "by your own figures, Mrs. Cool—now I don't want to trap you, but by your *own* figures, this Lidfield car was whirling around that intersection at a speed in excess of thirty-four miles per hour. Is that about right?"

Bertha said, "I don't think it was going that fast."

"Then your other testimony must have been wrong. Do you think that it was *more* than fifty feet from the intersection?"

"Well, not more."

"But at least fifty feet from the scene of the accident?"

"Yes."

"Then your time must have been wrong. You think it was more than a second?"

"Perhaps."

"But you have already stated positively that it was just one second, Mrs. Cool. Do you want to change *that* testimony?"

Bertha was sweating all over her forehead now. She said, "I don't know how fast the car was going. I just looked up and saw it and then there was a crash."

"Oh, you looked *up* and saw it!"

"Yes."

"Then you must have been looking *down* before the crash."

"Well, I don't know where I was looking."

"I see. You don't know whether your car was moving or whether it was stopped. You don't know whether you were looking to one side or looking to the other?"

"I was looking down," Bertha said.

"Then you weren't looking to one side."

"No."

"Then you couldn't have been looking at Esther Witson."

"I was looking at her."

"Make up your mind," Mysgart said.

Bertha remained doggedly silent.

Mysgart smiled triumphantly. "I think," he announced, "that is all."

The man who was taking down the record closed his shorthand notebook. Esther Witson smirked at Bertha and walked out. Mysgart scratched his nose with his mustache.

Swiftly the people thinned out until Bertha and I were alone once more in an office that seemed something like a prize ring after the contestants had left.

Chapter Fifteen

DONALD MOPS UP

BERTHA COOL CAREFULLY CLOSED THE DOOR. "Damn you," she said. "You got me into that. Why didn't you tell me what I was going up against?"

"I tried to, but you told me that no damn lawyer could rattle you."

Bertha just glared at me, reached for a cigarette.

I took one from my pocket and settled down into the client's chair.

Bertha said, "How the hell can anyone remember all those little things? You can't remember what you were doing and just how many seconds elapsed and all that sort of stuff."

I said, "I'm interested in Esther Witson. She'd been tagging along for eight or ten blocks. Now you remember she—"

There was a timid knock at the door.

I said, "If that happens to be Mysgart, don't lose your temper."

Bertha looked at me helplessly. "If it's that damn lawyer," she said, "you—you do the talking, lover."

I opened the door.

Mysgart said, "May I come in?"

"Come on in," I told him, and indicated the clients' chair.

Mysgart smiled at Bertha Cool. "I trust there are no hard feelings, Mrs. Cool."

I answered for Bertha. "No hard feelings," I told him. "It's all a matter of business."

"Thank you, Mr. Lam. I'm glad you appreciate my position. My client is a little impulsive—as so many women are."

Bertha simply glared at him, and blew smoke out through her nostrils.

"Cigarette?" I asked Mysgart.

"Thank you."

I passed over the humidor. He took one and lit it.

"Is Mrs. Lidfield badly injured?" I asked.

He made a little grimace and said, "You know how those things go. If she gets a settlement she'll be running around spry as can be. If she doesn't, she'll be in bed for a year. Glimson is a shrewd one. He specializes in this sort of stuff."

"You're no slouch, yourself," I told him.

He grinned.

Bertha said, "Of all the goddamn—"

I said to Bertha, "Excuse me. If *you're* going to handle it, I'll go out."

I started for the door.

"Don't go, Donald."

I hesitated a moment, looked meaningly at her.

"I'll keep quiet," Bertha promised.

I took my hand off the knob of the door.

Mysgart said hastily, "Mrs. Cool said something about being willing to effect a settlement in the case so she wouldn't have to be a witness."

"She's been a witness now," I said.

Mysgart opened his briefcase, fumbled around, brought out some papers, and started looking at them very studiously. He said, "I think it might be possible to settle the case. I think that's the reason Glimson wanted to rush ahead with these depositions. I think he wanted to get some kind of a settlement."

"Well," I said, "anything you want to make."

He looked at me in surprise. "You mean that you don't want to make any settlement now?"

"Not particularly."

"Why, Mr. Lam! I don't want to precipitate an argument, and I trust we can handle this in a business spirit and in a friendly way, but the evidence now shows that Mrs. Cool was quite negligent according to her own testimony. She was stopping at an illegal place, at an illegal time, in an illegal manner, and giving conflicting signals for two illegal maneuvers as well as this waving signal."

I said, "How about your own client? If Lidfield was driving his car fast then, he must have been in the intersection *before* Esther Witson entered the intersection. So then it was up to her to look out for him."

Mysgart said, "I will admit that there are some puzzling aspects to the case."

"They aren't puzzling Glimson any."

Mysgart sighed. "I was hoping," he said, "that a way would present itself by which we could get the entire matter cleared up."

"How much does Glimson want?"

"Oh, I haven't the faintest idea."

I kept on smoking.

"If you folks would make some contribution," Mysgart said, "my client might be prepared to make some contribution, and between us we might get the situation straightened up."

I said, "Why don't you quit beating around the bush?"

Mysgart scratched his nose with the red mustache. "The situation," he said, "has some unfortunate aspects."

I said, "All right. I'll break the ice. We'll give you five hundred dollars."

He looked at me reproachfully. "Five hundred dollars! Is that intended to be a joke—or an insult?"

I said, "You can take it either way. If you don't want it, I'll withdraw it."

"No, no. No, no," he said. "Now don't be hasty, Mr. Lam. After all, you and I are businessmen, and we can keep our tempers. Can't we?"

"I don't know," I told him.

Mysgart jumped up, shoving papers back in his brief-case. "Now just keep calm," he said. "Just keep cool, Mr. Lam. After all, you and I are businessmen. We'll see what we can do. Glimson and his client are waiting out by the elevator. I'll talk with him."

Mysgart went out the door.

"Why didn't you offer him fifteen hundred bucks?"

Bertha asked. "He'd have jumped at that."

I said, "Wait and see."

Bertha said, "The whole damn thing is screwy to me. Damn lawyers, anyway. I hate their guts. The questions that man asked me! Why, if a man jumped on you like that, you couldn't tell what you'd had for breakfast."

I grinned at her.

"Go on and grin like a Cheshire cat," Bertha said. "I'd just like to see you get up there on the witness stand once and let those birds start asking you questions."

The telephone rang.

Bertha pounced on the receiver, said, "Hello," and then made her voice all honey and syrup. "Oh yes, Miss Rushe. No *indeed*, we haven't forgotten you. Just a moment and I'll let you talk with Donald. He's around the office somewhere. It may take me a minute to get him. Just hold the line."

Bertha clapped her palm over the mouthpiece of the telephone and said, "It's Georgia Rushe and damned if I hadn't forgotten all about her. What are we supposed to be doing for her—oh, yes, that investigation of Mrs. Crail. It's up to you to talk to her, lover. You're good at making things up on the spur of the moment. Thank heavens I had sense enough to stall her along and tell her you weren't immediately available. Start thinking and I'll tell her that you're busy dictating and she'll have to wait a minute."

"I'll talk to her," I said.

"Well, think up something good," Bertha told me.

Bertha took her hand off the mouthpiece and said, "He's dictating, Miss Rushe, but he'll be here right away. He . . . Here he is now . . . What? What's that?"

Bertha scowled portentously into the mouthpiece. "Say that over again," she said. "Say it slow."

Bertha listened for as much as thirty seconds, then said, "You're sure that's what you want? Well, if that's the way you feel about it. Poor child, you're crying! Now listen. You better talk with Donald. He's here. He wants to talk with you."

Bertha once more clapped her palm over the mouth-piece.

"Take it, Donald. She's nuts, too!"

I took the telephone, said, "Lam talking, Miss Rushe."

Georgia Rushe poured words into the telephone with such rapidity that it was difficult to understand them. It was a steady stream of almost hysterical sound.

"I want you to call everything off, Mr. Lam. I want you to stop it. Don't do another thing. Let it go just as it is. I'm sorry I ever started it. I didn't realize what it would lead to or I wouldn't have done so. And don't worry about the two hundred dollars. Simply keep that and forget about the whole thing. Only don't—don't under any circumstances ever let on that I employed you to do anything. And please, please stop everything right now. Don't do another bit of work. Just stop whatever you're doing. Quit the whole business."

"May I ask why you've reached this decision, Miss Rushe?"

"I can't tell you. I can't tell you a thing in the world about it. I don't have time to discuss things. I don't want to. Just let it go, please."

I said, "Perhaps you'd better come into the office personally and confirm these instructions."

"You don't need them confirmed. They're all right. You do just as I tell you. Surely it doesn't need any signature before a notary public to tell you to quit work. What's the matter with you people? What are you trying to do, anyway? Just quit it. I tell you I want you to stop. Don't do another thing. Just forget the whole business. Keep the money. Stop right there."

She was keying herself up to a hysterical pitch.

"But, Miss Rushe, we're just beginning to get some really valuable information. We're getting—"

"That's what I was afraid of. That's why I want you to stop. Stop right now. I don't want anything more. I'm—I'm going away. I'm—I'm not going to be here. You won't see me again—ever."

I heard the sound of a choking sob at the other end of

the line, and then abruptly the receiver was hung up.

I dropped my receiver back into the cradle.

"What do you make of it?" Bertha asked.

I looked at Bertha gravely and said, "As nearly as *I* can make anything of it, she wants us to quit working on the case."

Red blood flushed into Bertha's face. "Damn it! Don't you think I can understand the English language? I know what she said. I was asking you what you made of it. At times you're the most despicable little—"

A timid knock sounded on the door.

"Mysgart," I said.

Bertha gave me a final glare, then put on her best receiving-a-client smile and said, "After all, the son-of-a-bitch is making money for us. Come in."

Mysgart opened the door almost apologetically. The way he moved into the room was an indication of the pussyfooting tactics in which he was indulging. The feet unconsciously adjusted themselves to the man's mental processes. He all but tiptoed over to the clients' chair. "Mr. Lam," he said, "I think that if you could make that one thousand dollars we could effect a settlement."

I looked at my watch and grinned at him. "You're just two minutes too late."

"What do you mean?"

I said, "I mean, Mrs. Cool and I have just received a very unpleasant jolt. A very important case on which we were working has been canceled."

"A big case?" he asked.

"It was a small case," I said, "as cases start. But it was leading to something big, very big."

Mysgart scratched his nose with his mustache.

I said, "Under the circumstances, I don't see how we can even contribute five hundred dollars toward a settlement. I'm afraid we'll have to just let the thing take its course."

"Oh, but you can't do that! You can't do that! I've already made the settlement!"

"On the basis of a thousand dollars?" I asked.

"Just a minute," he said. He came up out of the clients' chair with a rush. "Just a minute now. Don't go away! Just a minute now!"

He was out through the door like a fleeting shadow.

Bertha looked at me and said, "Whatever Georgia Rushe said over the telephone doesn't affect the job we are doing for Mr. Crail."

I said breezily, "Well, let's not be narrow-minded about it—particularly when we're dealing with an automobile lawyer."

Bertha batted her eyes at me, said suddenly, "I love you, you little bastard. I have the greatest admiration for the thinking machine that's back of your eyes—and you make me so goddamn mad I could kill you a dozen times a day. You—"

Mysgart's timid little knock sounded on the door, and this time he didn't wait for an invitation to enter, but having made the knock as a matter of formality, he twisted the knob, opened the door just far enough to accommodate his pudgy body, and slipped into the room, closing the door silently behind him. He was nodding his head. His lips were smiling, but his eyes were dubiously apprehensive.

"It's all right. I've got it fixed. It's all settled. My congratulations to both of you. You've worked out a very fine settlement. You've extricated yourselves from a very precarious position. It's all right. Five hundred dollars will do it. I've explained to the parties that the cash will be immediately forthcoming."

I said, "Mrs. Cool will want releases signed by Mr. Lidfield, Mrs. Lidfield, and Esther Witson."

"She shall have them. I've taken the liberty of asking your secretary to type out a release from Esther Witson, Mrs. Cool; and Mr. Glimson has the releases all signed by Mrs. Lidfield and Mr. Lidfield."

"Where did he get Mrs. Lidfield's signature?" Bertha asked suspiciously.

"Glimson had a signed release with him, the consideration, of course, being blank."

Bertha pushed back her chair an inch or two. "Do you mean the son-of-a-bitch came up here and put on that act for the sole purpose of blackmailing me into a settlement? You mean that he had the signed release in his briefcase all the time he—"

Mysgart held up a pudgy hand. "Just a moment, Mrs. Cool. Just a moment. Calm yourself, *please!* I beg of you, don't get all excited. It's not entirely an unusual situation. An attorney secures a written power of attorney from a client to effect a settlement, then has the client sign a release, the attorney being given a certain leeway, a certain discretion. That's so that when all of the parties are together and are in a mood for settlement, a prompt settlement can be put through without the necessity of a lot of delay which sometimes leads to complications. I can assure you that it's not at all unusual, Mrs. Cool. *I've even done it myself!*"

I said to Bertha Cool, "Make out a check to John Carver Mysgart, attorney for Esther Witson; and Cosgate & Glimson, attorneys for Mr. & Mrs. Rolland Lidfield, in an amount of five hundred dollars."

"What the hell are you talking about?" Bertha said. "I make out a check to the Lidfields and to Esther Witson, and I turn it over when I get the release and not before."

Mysgart coughed.

I said to Bertha, "No soap, Bertha. You're dealing with a couple of automobile lawyers."

"What the hell do you mean?" Bertha asked.

I said, "It's a matter of professional courtesy to make the check payable to the lawyer rather than the client."

"Then what protects me?"

"The release of the client," Mysgart interposed, smiling gratefully at me. "You have the signed release of the client, a release which will be ample in form, Mrs. Cool, releasing you from all claims of any sort, nature, or description from the beginning of the world to the date hereof."

"From the beginning of the world?" Bertha said.

Mysgart's bald head reflected the light as he nodded vehemently. "A legal form, Mrs. Cool, a safeguard."

"You're so good to me," Bertha said sarcastically and then added, "Fifty thousand years would be all right."

"The beginning of the world is a legal safeguard. It's a form, Mrs. Cool. Apparently Mr. Lam has some familiarity with the procedure in such cases, and I think he can assure you that it's a customary form and it would be well for you to take advantage of its protection."

"Oh, nuts!" Bertha said disgustedly. "Have I got to write all that stuff in a check?"

I said, "Elsie can type it. Give me a check and I'll go out and get her to fill it in."

"Don't give up the check until you get the releases," Bertha said.

Mysgart coughed again.

I said to Mysgart, "The bank's right downstairs. It's after hours, but we can get in the side door and they'll cash a check given for a settlement like this. You and Glimson can go down to the bank with me. When the cashier shoves the cash through the window you and Glimson can hand me the signed releases, and—"

Mysgart's head was bobbing enthusiastically up and down. "You and I are businessmen, Mr. Lam! That's excellent."

Bertha jerked open the drawer of the desk, pulled out a checkbook, and ripped out a blank check which she fairly shoved into my hand. "Donald," she said, "if you love me, get these goddamn lawyers out of my office."

Mysgart turned and started to say something conciliatory.

I slipped my hand through his arm and gently led him out of the office.

Elsie Brand had to crowd the lines in order to get all of that in the check, but she managed it.

I said to Mysgart, "Wait here. I'll go and get Bertha's signature on the check, then we'll go downstairs. Now there's a couple of things we'll want in connection with the settlement."

"What are those?"

I said, "Esther Witson was a busy little woman getting names and license numbers of witnesses at the time of the accident, and I think Mr. Lidfield did a little prowling around on his own. My partner is a little suspicious. She'll want to get all of the data that both parties had, the names of witnesses and license numbers."

"Oh, yes," Mysgart said, nodding enthusiastically once more. "I can appreciate her attitude. She confuses my professional attitude with my personal relations. She shall have all the data, Lam, all of it. We won't hold out a thing. No, indeed!"

He beamed at me.

I took the check in and put it on Bertha's desk.

She looked at me suspiciously, said, "When these goddamn lawyers start pussyfooting around the office and smirking at each other, damned if you don't join in the procession and pussyfoot and smirk right along with the rest of them. I don't know what the hell it is. It's probably your legal training."

Bertha grabbed up the desk pen and all but jabbed the point through the paper as she signed the check.

I went out, gently closing the door.

The little group was clustered around the elevator. Lidfield came over and thrust out a rather timid hand. "I haven't had a chance to meet you, Mr. Lam. I'm glad we're getting this thing settled. Rather a nasty case."

"I only hope your wife will get better," I said.

A look of ineffable sadness crossed his face. "I hope so. Poor girl!"

We all went down to the bank.

"Now just a moment," I said, "before the money is passed over. You'll remember that I was to get a complete list of the witnesses."

Mysgart smiled at Esther Witson and said, "That was the understanding, Miss Witson. I think you have a notebook there—"

Esther Witson pulled a notebook out of her pocket, said, "You can copy these or—"

I said, "Just take the original pages out of the notebook. It's a loose-leaf notebook and—"

Esther Witson jerked the pages out of the notebook and handed them to me.

"These are all?" I asked.

"All," she said.

"Now then," Glimson said, "there's a consideration to be paid by Miss Witson herself, and—"

"We can do that between us," Mysgart interposed hurriedly. "Miss Witson's bank is down the street four or five blocks, and if we hurry, we'll be able to get in the side door. They know Miss Witson very well down there, and—"

Glimson said to Lidfield, "Give me a list of your witnesses."

Lidfield was rather apologetic. He said, "I just wrote the license number of every car that was around there that I could see."

I said to Glimson, "Of course after your client gave you the license numbers of these automobiles, you had them investigated and have the names of the owners?"

Glimson sighed reluctantly, opened his briefcase, and took out a typewritten sheet of paper which he handed to me without a word.

The teller looked at me inquiringly.

I nodded.

They grabbed the money and started for the door of the bank, anxious to get down to Esther Witson's bank while they could still get in.

Chapter Sixteen

THE ONE WHO GETS HURT

I CROSSED OVER TO A PHONE BOOTH and telephoned the office. Elsie Brand answered the telephone.

"Hello, Elsie." I asked, "How's the blood pressure?"

"Pretty high."

"Okay. I've got a little thinking to do. If there'll be a rise in blood pressure in the office I'll go over and sit in the car while I think things out."

"Personally," Elsie said, "I'd recommend the car. The open air will be restful. There still seems to be the question of where you were last night."

"Okay. Thanks. Be a good girl."

"It seems almost compulsory," she said, and hung up before I could ask her what she meant by that crack.

I went across to the parking-lot, sat in the agency car, and took out the loose-leaf notebook pages I'd received from Esther Witson in connection with the settlement.

The name of Mrs. Crail wasn't on there. The name of Rufus Stanberry wasn't on there. The name of Boskovitche wasn't on there. That whole page of the notebook was missing. There were half a dozen other names and license numbers. I put them to one side for a minute and looked at the list I'd got from Lidfield.

These were just license numbers, but on the typewritten sheet which Glimson had passed over, these license numbers were listed against names of registered owners.

There was the license number of Bertha Cool's car; Bertha Cool's name and address; the license number of a car listed as belonging to Mrs. Ellery Crail, 1013 Scarabia Boulevard; a license number of a car listed as a Cadillac sedan registered to Rufus Stanberry, 3271 Fulrose Avenue; three or four license numbers that checked with those on the Esther Witson list; a couple of license numbers that Esther Witson didn't have; then a license number, *Miss Georgia Rushe, 207 West Orleans Avenue*.

I folded the list, put it in my wallet, crossed over to a telephone, and rang the Crail Venetian Blind Company. "May I speak with Miss Georgia Rushe?" I asked the switchboard operator.

"Who wants to speak with her? You'll have to give your name."

"Tell her Donald wants to talk with her."

"Just a moment."

I heard the plugging of connections, the distant echoes of a ghostly voice, then the professionally cordial voice characteristic of a high-class switchboard operator said, "She went home early tonight."

I looked at my watch. It was four thirty-five.

"Thank you," I said and hung up.

I tried Georgia Rushe at the phone number she'd left with us when she'd employed us. There was no answer.

I went back to the agency car and warmed up the motor while I was making a mental check of times and places, getting the sequence of events straightened out in my own mind.

Then I drove to the Crail Venetian Blind Company.

The building was a big three-story brick structure down on the fringe of the commercial district. The sign over the door was old and grimy. Gilt letters that had been on there for a long time said: *Crail Venetian Blind Company*.

I parked the car near the entrance. It was past quitting time and a straggling stream of workers was filing out—older men carrying lunch pails, slim, attractive girls gushing with the healthy vitality of youth, chatting gaily as they moved down the stairs.

I walked in and tried the inner door. It was locked with a spring lock. I stood by it waiting until a girl, hurrying to catch up with a group down the street, flung it open. She hardly noticed me as I caught the door and prevented the latch from clicking.

A sign said: *Offices Up Stairs,* and I climbed the stairs

into a little reception room where there was a counter, a few chairs, and a little arched opening in a partition bearing the word: *Information*. Below this was a glass door which could be swung open and shut so that a person standing on the other side of the counter couldn't hear confidential communications which took place over the inside phone.

There seemed to be no one back of the arched opening, so I walked around to a gate in the partition, found one of those trick catches which are released by an electro-magnet from the inside or a pressure of the fingers in the right place, pushed up the catch, opened the gate, and went in.

There was a long hallway with half-glassed partitions bearing signs in gilt letters: *Sales Manager, Credit Manager, Accounting Office,* and down at the far end a door marked: *President.* Up here in this corridor there was no sound save the noises of occasional activity from the floor below—steps, the banging of a door, the sound of a voice. The second floor itself was silent as a deserted courtroom after the defendant had been sentenced to death and the judge has gathered his papers and gone out to play golf.

I pushed open the door marked, *President.*

Ellery Crail sat at his desk, his chin over on his chest, his big competent hairy hands clinched so tightly that the afternoon light which filtered in from the big window touched the taut skin over the knuckles into high lights.

He didn't hear the door open, and he didn't look up. He was staring with steady-eyed concentration, his face dark with tortured thought. He might have been hypnotized, sitting there in the rigid immobility of a trance.

I walked across the thick carpet. And it wasn't until I was seating myself in the chair opposite the desk that he saw me, looked up with a frown of annoyance, and then as recognition flooded his features said with sudden irritation, "You!"

I nodded.

"How did you get in?"

"Walked in."

"That door's supposed to be locked."

I said, "Let's get in touch with Georgia Rushe."

"She isn't here. She left early. She's gone home."

I said, "She's taking a powder."

It took a moment or two for the full effect of my words to dawn on him. Then he said, "Powder! Good Heavens, Lam, not that!"

I said, "I was using a slang expression of the underworld. It means skipping out—taking what is known as a runout powder."

"Good God, I thought you meant—"

"What?"

"I didn't know what you meant."

"Poison?"

"Perhaps."

I said, "Let's go have a talk with her. In case you don't know the address, it's two-o-seven West Orleans Avenue. I have my car downstairs."

He looked at me for a second or two, his eyes hitting me with a hard, flinty impact. "How much," he asked, "do *you* know?"

"So much you don't have to say anything you don't want to."

Without a word he pushed back his chair. "All right," he said, "let's go."

We went down the wide stairs and out through the locked door. A watchman was now on duty, and he said mechanically, "Good night, Mr. Crail."

"Good night, Tom," Crail said.

The door closed behind us and the lock clicked into place. I indicated the agency car with a jerk of my thumb and said, "That's it."

I went around to the driver's seat and Crail climbed into the front seat beside me. We encountered quite a bit of traffic at that hour, but I was taking chances on a ticket and was less than ten minutes getting to 207 West Orleans Avenue.

It was an old-fashioned apartment house with no attempt at the white stucco exterior which is so frequently used to hide the grime of drab age. A few straggling green vines grew up the front of the building. The narrow windows told their own stories of insufficient light and ventilation. One look at the place and you could smell the psychic stench of dejected spirits, the physical odors of ancient cooking, the irritating fumes of defective gas heaters.

I held back slightly and Crail led the way.

His finger found the button opposite a piece that had been cut from a calling card printed in Old English lettering, *Georgia Rushe.*

Nothing happened.

The lock on the outer door was a little better than most of them. I had a passkey I thought would fit it, but I didn't want to show my hand just then. I pressed two or three buttons at random and, after a moment, there was the distinctive buzz from the inside which indicated that someone was pressing a button which controlled the electric catch on the door.

I pushed the entrance door open.

The number on Georgia Rushe's mailbox showed that her apartment was 243. There may have been an elevator in the back part of the hall, but I didn't wait for it. I started climbing the stairs and Crail, climbing with the effort of a heavily muscled man, came lunging along behind me. I took the stairs two at a time.

No one answered when I knocked on apartment 243.

I looked at Crail. His face was drawn and haggard. Even in the dim light of the stuffy, smelly hallway, I could see the dead white pallor of his skin and the deep lines that etched themselves down from his nostrils to the corners of his mouth.

I saw no reason for being namby-pamby about it. I took a leather key container from my pocket, slid back the zipper, and shook out my skeleton keys.

The first one did the trick. The lock clicked back and we went in.

It was near the back of the building on the north side. A little single apartment that had two narrow windows that furnished a small amount of ventilation. The only cross ventilation was through an adjustable transom over the top of the door.

A light was on in the apartment, and the globe was powerful enough to make the room seem rather bright. It was a conventional single apartment with a disappearing wall bed behind a glass-knobbed gray painted door. The overstuffed chair had seen better days and the upholstery had been pounded down with use until it was hard and lumpy. The davenport had probably been refinished a couple of times and was in need of a third treatment. The faded carpet was worn almost through to the floor by the table, and two deep circles marked where the foot of the bed would rest when it was lowered. A drawer was open in a little all-purpose table which would, at night, be by the side of the bed. A pine table stained a dark mahogany was in the center of the room. On it were a few magazines.

A woman's hat and coat lay on a chair. The door of what had once been a closet was wide open to disclose a little sink and a two-burner gas stove over which was a small-sized electric refrigerator and a shelf containing a few dishes and glasses. A door which had a built-in full-length mirror was evidently the door to the bathroom.

On a straight-backed chair was a suitcase about half packed, the lid being raised to disclose the feminine garments on the interior.

Crail heaved a deep sigh of relief. "She hasn't left yet," he said.

I looked the place over and said, "Whenever the management goes to the extent of putting in brilliant light globes, you know the place is dark as hell in the daytime," and switched out the lights.

Instantly the place became dark, gloomy, and depressing. What afternoon light filtered in through the window was so badly dispersed that it gave the place an atmosphere of gloomy unreality.

I noticed a knifelike ribbon of light coming from under the door of the bathroom.

Crail said, "For God's sake, switch that light back on."

I clicked the switch.

"Well," Crail said, "she's probably gone out to get something. She's packing. I guess we—"

"What *do* we do?"

"Wait."

I said, "Okay, sit down."

Crail took the lumpy overstuffed chair and tried to fidget himself into a position that was comfortable.

I walked over to the occasional table which would be by the head of the bed when the bed was let down, and looked in the open drawer.

There was a small bottle in there with the cap unscrewed. The bottle was empty. The label said: *Luminal.*

I thought for a moment, looked at my watch, then said to Crail, "What time did she leave the office?"

"About four-ten," Crail said. "She said she wasn't feeling well and wanted to go home. I told her to go ahead."

I said, "Did you notice anything peculiar?"

"About what?"

"About the way she said good-by."

He looked at me with tortured eyes, then nodded his head slowly.

I didn't ask him what it was, but he volunteered the information. "There was a certain feeling in the way she said it. Something of finality. I guess she read my mind."

I looked at my watch. It was five-fifteen.

I sat down in a chair opposite Crail and took out a package of cigarettes. "Want one?" I asked.

He shook his head.

I lit a cigarette, and Crail sat watching me. The hundred-watt light in the ceiling showed small, almost microscopic beads of perspiration on his forehead.

"How," Crail asked, "did you happen to know—that she was going, I mean."

I looked at him and said, "How did you happen to

know that your wife had been driving behind Rufus Stanberry?"

His eyes shifted for a moment, then came back to mine. "She told me."

I grinned at him.

His face flushed. "You don't believe it?"

"No."

His mouth tightened. "I'm not accustomed to having my word questioned."

"I know," I said sympathetically. "Lying comes hard to you. Was Georgia driving her car, or did you borrow it?"

He couldn't keep the consternation out of his eyes.

I settled back in my chair and puffed on the cigarette.

"How did you know Georgia's car was there?" he asked.

"One of the parties to the automobile accident took down the license numbers of a whole flock of automobiles."

He said, "They must have got the wrong license number."

I smiled and said nothing.

"All right," Crail blurted, "I borrowed her car. She didn't know anything about it. I—I mean what I wanted it for. I—damn it, Lam, I was such a despicable cad that I followed my wife. I wanted to know—well, I thought she had an engagement to meet someone, and I wondered—well, you know, that Stanberry Building."

"I know," I said.

He didn't say anything for a while.

I said, "When you realized your wife was in trouble, you decided that it didn't make any difference what it was, you were going to stand by her. But you knew that Esther Witson had got her name and address as well as the license number of the car in connection with that automobile accident, so you wanted it settled."

He didn't say anything.

I said, "Life is a peculiar phenomenon, or rather a whole series of phenomena. Lots of times it's hard to do something without hurting someone."

I saw him look at me searchingly, but I kept my profile to him and kept on talking abstractly. "Lots of times, in affairs of the heart, you have to hurt either one person or another no matter what you do. Sometimes you hurt several people. But when you have to choose the person you don't want to hurt, you sometimes get hypnotized into choosing the person who doesn't want to be hurt. Do you get what I mean?"

"I don't see what this has to do with it," he said.

I said, "Sometimes a woman who really loves you will remain in the background so that you don't realize the full extent to which you are hurting her. On the other hand, there are lots of women who are adept at putting it up to you in terms of 'I don't want to be hurt.' "

"What the hell are you talking about?" Crail asked.

"Your wife," I said, and stopped talking.

There was a long ten seconds of silence.

"By God!" Crail said in a choking voice, and got to his feet.

I didn't say anything.

"I should hit you," he said.

"Don't do it," I told him. "Go look in the bathroom instead."

Crail gave me one tortured, anguished look. Then he got to the bathroom door in three steps and jerked it open.

Georgia Rushe was lying in the bathtub, fully clothed. Her eyes were closed. Her face was slightly pallid and her jaw was dropped.

I crossed over to the telephone, dialed Police Headquarters, and said, "Connect me with Frank Sellers of Homicide—quick!"

It was only a couple of seconds before I had Sellers on the line.

"Frank," I said, "this is Donald Lam. Send an ambulance to two-o-seven West Orleans Avenue. The party you want is in apartment two-forty-three. She's tried to commit suicide by taking Luminal. It hasn't been over forty-five minutes since she took the dose and a stomach pump and stimulant should fix her up."

"What's her name?" Sellers asked.

"Georgia Rushe."

"Why do I bother with it?"

I said, "Ellery Crail is here and he'll have a story to tell you if you talk to him about it."

"I get you."

I said, "And have one of your men get hold of Frank L. Glimson of Cosgate & Glimson. They're lawyers. Tell Glimson that Irma Begley, who was the plaintiff in a case against Philip E. Cullingdon, has confessed to fraud and has made statements that implicate Cosgate & Glimson. Ask them if they care to make any statements. And keep them away from the telephone."

"This Georgia Rushe," Sellers said, "will she talk?"

"No. The party *you* want is Ellery Crail."

Crail, just emerging from the bathroom, said, "What's that? Who's mentioning my name?"

I said, "I was trying to get some hot coffee sent up. We'd better get her out of the bathtub and see if we can put some cold water on her."

I hung up.

Crail and I lifted her out of the bathtub.

"She's drugged!" Crail said. "We've got to do something!"

I said, "Put some cold towels on her forehead and on her chest. I tried to get some hot coffee sent up, but they won't send it. I'm going down and bring up some black coffee."

Crail looked desperately at the kitchen and said, "Perhaps we can make some coffee here."

"We haven't time. There's a restaurant down the street," I said, and bolted out of the door, leaving Crail behind with Georgia Rushe.

Chapter Seventeen

DOUBLE PINCH

I DROVE THE AGENCY CAR FAST, taking chances on a speeding ticket. It would have been a good plan to have parked it a block or two away from Billy Prue's apartment, but I didn't have the time. I drove right up to the apartment house, parked the car in front of the door, ran up the steps, and rang Billy Prue's bell.

It was one chance in ten—one chance in a hundred. If she was there at all, she would be packing up, but— I rang the bell again.

Nothing happened.

The lock on the outer door was pretty well worn. Any key that would fit the grooves would work the lock. I didn't even have to bother with my skeleton keys. The key to my own apartment worked the lock on the outer door.

I went up to Billy Prue's apartment. I knocked on the door twice. There was no sound from the interior. The place was thick with silence.

I took out my skeleton keys and tried one in the lock. It didn't work.

Before I could take it out, the door was jerked open from the inside.

Billy Prue said sarcastically, "Make yourself right at home! Walk right in— Oh, it's *you!*"

"Why don't you answer a knock on your door?" I asked her.

Her hand went up to her throat. She said, "You scared the living daylights out of me."

"You didn't act like it."

"I didn't dare to. Why didn't you say who it was?"

"How could I?"

"You could have called through the door."

I carefully closed the door behind me and made sure

that the spring lock clicked into place. I said, "That would have been nice—stand out in the hall and yell, 'Yoo-hoo, Billy, this is Donald Lam, the private detective. I want to see you on business. Open up!'"

"Oh," she said, "on *business,* is it?" .

I looked around the room. The door to the bedroom was open. The bed was pretty well covered with folded clothes. There were two big suitcases and a steamer trunk on the floor, also a couple of hat boxes.

"Going somewhere?" I asked.

"You wouldn't expect me to stay *here,* would you?"

"Not if you could find some other place."

"I've found another place."

"Where?"

"With a friend."

I said, "Sit down for a minute. We've got to talk."

"I want to get out of here, Donald. It's terribly depressing and—and I'm afraid!"

"What are you afraid of?"

She hastily averted her eyes. "Nothing."

"Delightfully logical," I said.

"Shut up. You don't have to be logical when you're afraid."

"Perhaps not."

I stretched out in a comfortable chair, lit a cigarette, and said, "Let's talk some sense."

"What about?"

"About the murder."

"Do we have to talk about it?"

"Yes."

"What about it?"

"You're absolutely certain his watch was an hour fast when you left?"

"Yes."

"And you set it back an hour when you returned?"

"Yes."

"You're sure you didn't set it back an hour *before?*"

"No, and I should have. That bothered me because I was supposed to have done so."

I said, "All right. Let's use our heads. Two people tampered with that watch. You were one of them. Now then, how many people knew about the plan to set the watch ahead?"

"Just Pittman Rimley and I."

"And the boy in the washroom."

"Yes, I forgot about him."

I got out of the chair and paced the floor for a minute or so. She sat perfectly still, watching me, not saying a word.

I walked over to the windows and stood looking down at the street below.

"What are you looking at?"

"The agency car parked down there in front of the place."

She came to stand at my side. "What about it?"

I said, "Somebody put the murder weapon in there yesterday. I don't know when it was put in, so I've got to start figuring *why* it was put in, because that may give me a clue to *when*."

She said, "What do you mean *why*? You mean someone was trying to frame you?"

I said, "Either someone wanted to frame me, or someone didn't."

"That's elemental."

I said, "We have to begin with elemental facts. There's one explanation that's so damn simple that I've overlooked it."

"What?"

I said, "Either someone put that weapon in my car because he wanted to frame me, or he didn't. Naturally, I've acted on the assumption that whoever put it in there wanted to frame me. I'm beginning to think about the simple explanation now."

"What?"

I said, "Let's make another division. Whoever put that weapon in the car either knew it was my car, or didn't."

"Good heavens, Donald, you don't think there's the

slightest possibility anyone put it in your car simply by accident?"

"Not by accident. That's taxing credulity altogether too much."

She said, "I don't get you. You seem to be contradicting yourself."

"No, there's one other explanation."

"What?"

I said, "The weapon was put in my car because my car happened to be the most convenient place to hide the thing."

"Oh, oh!" she said as the full implication of that dawned on her.

"So," I said, "I keep thinking back where my car was. Where would it have been parked sufficiently soon after the murder so that someone would find it the most convenient place to dispose of the murder weapon?"

She said eagerly, "Donald, you *may* have something there."

I said, "How about Pittman Rimley, can you trust him?"

"So far he's always been on the square—with me."

"There were two persons who knew about the watch business—Rimley and the man in the washroom. Then there was a third person who could have known."

"Who?"

"Mrs. Crail. Stanberry might have commented on the time to her. That's logical, isn't it?"

"It is when you put it that way."

I said, "And I'm wondering why the handle of the hand ax had been sawed off. You've used a meat saw?"

"Yes—of course."

"One here in the apartment?"

"I guess so, yes."

"Let's get it out and take a look at it."

She regarded me thoughtfully for a moment, then went to the kitchenette. I followed her. The meat saw was under the sink. She handed it to me.

There was some grease on the blade and embedded

between the handle and the blade a few grains of saw-dust.

"That does it," I said.

"Does what?"

"Clinches the case."

"I don't see why."

I looked at her steadily. "You had a hand ax here, didn't you?"

Her eyes shifted.

I said, "Whoever did the job didn't expect to find Stanberry unconscious. When she did, and found a hand ax—well, that was it."

"She?"

"Yes. It was a woman."

I kept looking at her. "She didn't want to leave the murder weapon here. She had only one way of taking it out—in her handbag. She had to saw a piece off the handle to make it fit."

"Donald!"

I turned to look down at the street. For several seconds the apartment was silent. Then I said, "I'm still toying with the explanation that the murder weapon was ditched in my car simply because my car happened to be the most convenient place for the murderer to put the weapon. Now then, if we're going to work on *that* hypothesis, we suddenly find outselves up against—"

I broke off.

"What's the matter?" she asked.

"See that car?" I said.

She looked where I was pointing. "It's a police car," I said. "See the red spotlight—?"

Sergeant Frank Sellers got out of the car, gallantly walked around the car to the right side, opened the door, and held out his hand.

Bertha Cool put her hand on Frank Sellers's and got out of the car about as gracefully as a sack of sugar tumbling down off the top shelf in the pantry.

I said, "Quick! Get out of here and—! No, it's too late."

Bertha had spotted the agency car. I saw her tap Sellers on the shoulder and point. Sellers went over and looked at the license number. They talked together earnestly for a minute, then moved toward the door of the apartment house.

A moment later Billy Prue's bell made noise.

"What do I do?" she asked.

She was looking at me with eyes that were wells of dismay.

"Sit down in that chair," I said. "Don't move! Don't make a sound no matter *what* happens. Do you promise?"

"If you want me to."

"No matter what happens! Understand?"

"Yes. Anything you say, Donald."

The bell didn't make any more noise.

I opened the door to the corridor, made certain the spring lock was working. "No matter what happens, don't make a sound. Understand?"

She nodded.

I stepped out into the hall and pulled the door closed, dropped down on my hands and knees, and put my ear to the crack along the floor.

I was in that position when I heard faint steps down the corridor. I moved slightly, and the steps suddenly stopped.

I got to one knee, felt in my pocket for my collection of skeleton keys, took them out, and tried out one on the lock.

The steps sounded again.

I whirled with the guilty start of someone who has been detected in an unlawful activity.

Sergeant Sellers was right on top of me.

"So," he said, "got a key to the joint, have you?"

I tried to whip the keys back into my pocket.

Sergeant Sellers's fingers clamped my wrist.

"Well, well, well," Sellers said as his other hand snapped the key container out of my nerveless grasp. "So your agency plays around with skeleton keys, does it,

Bertha?"

Bertha said, "Damn you, Donald, I told you a long while ago to get rid of those. They'll get you in trouble."

I didn't say anything.

"What," Sellers asked, "is the big idea?"

I said, "I wanted to get in for a look around."

"I gathered you did. How long have you been here?"

"I don't know—four or five minutes, maybe."

"That long?"

I said, "I rang the bell three or four times to make sure there was no answer, then I—well, I got in through the outer door."

"Then what?"

"Then I came up here and knocked. Then I listened for quite a while. I didn't want to take chances on going in until I was sure the place was empty."

"It's empty?" Sellers asked.

"Yes. I think she moved out."

"Then why did you want in?"

"I wanted to check something about the position of the bathtub."

"Why?"

"I wanted to see where two people would have to stand if they lifted the body into the bathtub. It would take two men to—"

"Don't kid yourself," Sellers interrupted. "I've busted the case wide open."

"You have!"

"Yes. I want that jane."

"Why?"

"We've identified the hand ax. She bought it at a hardware store three blocks down the street."

I tried to make my voice sound unconcerned. "She's probably at the Rendezvous now. You didn't go out on that ambulance case?"

He grinned. "I thought that *could* have been a red herring, Donald. I wanted this Prue girl."

"But someone went out to that Orleans address?"

"Sure."

"And they won't let Crail get away?"

"No, sweetheart, and you won't get away, either. Come on. We're going places."

"Do I get my keys back?"

"Naughty, naughty."

"Take the damn things and throw them away," Bertha said angrily. "I've warned the little devil about that."

Sellers said, "Come on, quit stalling."

I followed them down to the street. I said, "I'll take the agency car and—"

"The hell you will!" Sellers said. "You'll stay right here, my lad, until I've put the bracelets on that little girl's wrists. You won't pull any slick little job of getting in to a telephone and tipping her off—"

"The bracelets on *her* wrists!"

"Sure. What did you think?"

"Don't let him stall you," Bertha said. "He knows. He's a smart little bastard. He was going to tip her off. My God, how he falls for women! That's the trouble with him."

Sellers said, "Listen, Donald, she's the one who did the killing. Don't get tangled up in it."

I looked at him and laughed. "Anyone could have picked up the hand ax," I said.

Sellers rose to the bait. "I've got the deadwood on her. Under an assumed name she rented an apartment in the Fulrose Apartments. She's had it for a month, always being careful never to go in except when Rufus Stanberry was out. She's been searching his apartment. The day of the murder, just after Stanberry had been bumped off, she showed up and made a good job of it. She went through the safe that time."

"How do you know?"

"Archie Stanberry tells me some things are missing from the safe."

"But how do you know *she* did it?"

He laughed and said, "She was smart when it came to going through Stanberry's apartment. She didn't leave any fingerprints. But she wasn't smart when she lived in that apartment under an assumed name. Hell, it wouldn't have done her any good anyway. She couldn't have lived there for a month without leaving finger-prints."

"You mean you've found her fingerprints in that apartment?"

"Sure. The one she rented under an assumed name. What's more, the manager and one of the clerks identify her photograph absolutely."

"Gosh!" I said.

"Don't let it get you, lover," Bertha said cheerfully. "She never was anything but a little gold digger with pretty legs."

"How did you get wise?" I asked Sellers.

"Shucks, there was nothing to it. You went out to see this man Cullingdon. She went out to see Cullingdon. Your cars were parked side by each, or end to end —whichever you want to call it. She knew where your car was. She knew whose car it was. You let her drive you away. After you left her, she had ample time to drive out and ditch the murder weapon in your car. She thought she was being smart as hell when she did it. It was one of those things that looked good at the time, but it stuck her head in the noose."

Bertha said suddenly, "Listen, Frank, I don't want to go back with you after you've made the pinch and have Donald in the car with that little tart. Suppose Donald and I take the agency car and follow right along behind you. I'll see that he doesn't telephone."

Sellers thought that over for a moment and said, "Okay."

He walked over to the agency car with me.

I reached in my pocket for the keys. A sinking feeling developed in the pit of my stomach. I'd left the car keys and my driving-gloves on the table in Billy Prue's apart-ment.

"Well?" Bertha said.

I know now how people feel when they get stage fright. There probably wasn't anything I could have said then that would have stalled the thing off, but if there had been, I couldn't have said it. I was absolutely tongue-tied. I just stood there fumbling through my pockets.

"Where are they?" Bertha said.

"I must have dropped them there on the carpet when I took these other keys out of my pocket."

Bertha looked at Frank Sellers.

Frank Sellers said softly under his breath, "Why, you dirty double-crosser!"

The next second I felt his left hand grab my wrist. I saw the flash of steel and heard the ratchet of handcuffs. Steel bit into my wrists.

"All right, wise guy," Sellers said. "I gave you a chance and you couldn't take it the easy way. You have to do it the hard way. All right, that's the way we're going to play from now on. Come on, buddy, you're going back upstairs."

I said indignantly, "What the hell's eating you? Those keys are somewhere there on the carpet in front of that door and—"

"And I've just noticed," Sellers said, "that you aren't wearing your driving gloves. A hell of a detective I am. Come on, buddy, we're going back."

We went back. There was nothing else to do.

Sellers got down on his knees in front of the door to Billy Prue's apartment. He felt along the carpet. It was only a perfunctory gesture. Then he took my own skeleton keys and fitted one into the lock.

I made one last desperate attempt.

"Are you going in there without a search warrant?" I asked.

Frank Sellers isn't a guy you can bluff that easy. "You're damn right I'm going in there without a warrant," he said.

The key clicked the lock back.

Billy Prue was sitting just as I had left her in the chair; her face might have been molded in pastry dough and daubed with make-up.

Sellers took in the situation with a practiced eye, walked over to the table, and said, "Those your gloves, Lam?"

I said, "I'm not answering any questions."

Sellers picked up the car keys, said, "The gloves and the keys will be evidence. Get your things on, Billy. You're going places. Let me see your hand a minute."

He picked up her hand.

There was nothing I could do about it even if I had warned her.

A half-second later she jerked back and screamed as the cold steel touched her wrists, then the ratchet bit into pressure and Billy Prue and I were handcuffed one to the other.

"All right, Little Miss Murderess and Mr. Accessory-After-the-Fact," Frank Sellers said grimly. "We're going to teach you little lovebirds something."

Bertha looked from me to Frank Sellers. "Listen, Frank," she said, "suppose—"

"Nothing doing," Sellers said roughly.

"But Frank—"

"Shut up," he said. "And this time, we *all* ride in my car."

Chapter Eighteen

U Turn

SELLERS ONLY STOPPED LONG ENOUGH to fit my keys to the lock on the agency car to make sure they worked. Then he loaded us into the police automobile, turned on the motor, and kicked in the siren.

It was a hell of a place in which to have to think, but I knew that I had to think, and think fast. By the time we reached Headquarters, it would be too late to do any good.

The siren was screaming for the right of way and the car was building into speed. We flashed past a street intersection. My eyes noticed the name of the street we were on. It was Mantica Street.

Ahead of us and on the left was a rather swanky apartment hotel. A couple of taxicabs were parked in front. One of the drivers looked up curiously as the siren went screaming by. I had a glimpse of a twisted, broken nose.

The next street was Garden Vista Boulevard and Frank Sellers was bracing his car for a screaming turn.

"Frank!" I yelled at him.

He didn't even turn his head.

The tires screamed the car around the turn.

"Frank, for God's sake stop!"

Something in my voice caught his ears, made him ease his foot on the throttle. "What is it this time, a stall?"

"The murderer of Rufus Stanberry," I said.

"I've got her right here."

"No, no, Frank. For God's sake—at least pull in to the curb and let me talk to you before he gets away."

He hesitated.

Bertha said, "Please, Frank."

"The hell with him," Frank said. "It's just a stall and you know it as well as I do. He's quick-witted enough to have thought up some lie and—"

"Goddammit!" Bertha screamed at him. "Pull this car in to the curb!"

Sellers looked at her in surprise.

Bertha leaned forward, twisted the ignition key in the lock, jerked it out, and held her hand out of the window.

The motor went dead. The momentum carried us in to the curb as Sellers turned the steering-wheel.

Sellers sat perfectly still. His face was white with rage.

After a half-second, he said in a choked voice, "It's all right with me. I take in the three of you."

Bertha looked back at me and said, "And don't kid yourself he isn't man enough to do it. If you've got anything to say, say it—and I hope to hell you've got something."

I leaned forward to put my left hand on Frank Sellers's shoulders. The right was handcuffed to Billy Prue.

"Listen, Frank," I said, "I'm coming clean. I've wondered how the hell that murder weapon got in my car. I've thought back over every step of the way. It couldn't, simply couldn't have been put in my car by someone who knew whose car it was and was framing things on me unless Billy Prue double-crossed me, and I don't think she double-crossed me. There's only one other way it could have got in my car."

Sellers was listening now.

I said, "Listen, Frank, I'm doing this for you as much as for anybody. For the love of Mike, don't pull us in and get a splash in the newspapers and then have to hide your face."

"Don't worry about *my* face," Sellers said. "Tell me about that murder weapon."

I said, "The only way it could have been put in the car was by someone who didn't know what car it was—who it belonged to."

"Nuts!" Sellers said.

"And," I went on, "there was only one way *that* could have happened and that was that my car happened to be the most convenient and the most accessible place for the murderer to have put it, and there's only one way *that* could have happened, and that was when my car was parked at the Rimley Rendezvous and I tried to be a smart aleck and squeeze in in front of the car behind me on the hope that it wouldn't go out before I did. But the guy in the car behind me wasn't that sort of an egg. He simply stuck his car in low gear and pushed mine out into the taxi zone and went on his way. And a taxi driver damn near beat me up over it when I came out—and that taxi driver was sitting in a cab at that hotel a couple of blocks back on Mantica Street. That's probably his regular stand. And the handle of that hand ax had been sawed off so it would fit in a woman's handbag."

"And what the hell's all that got to do with this pinch?" Sellers asked.

"Don't you see?" I said. "Don't you get the sketch? Remember that accident at Mantica Street and Garden Vista Boulevard? Figure out the time element. Now then, if you want to be a smart dick—be smart, and if you want to be dumb—be dumb. I've said everything I'm going to say. Put the keys back in the ignition, Bertha."

Bertha said, "But I don't get it, lover. What the hell has the taxicab got to do with—"

"Put the keys back in the lock," I said. "Sellers has a chance now to either cover himself with glory, or make himself the prize damn fool of the force."

Sellers said, "I'm not making myself a prize damn fool of anything—not with the stuff I've got on this Billy Prue."

"You haven't got a damn thing on her except coincidence," I went on. "Billy and I were having an affair before I left. She knew I was coming back. I couldn't be with her in the apartment where she was living without having Pittman Rimley blow my guts out. She got this apartment in the Fulrose Apartments so we could be together. It was a love nest. That's where I was last night, and why Bertha couldn't find me."

"You son-of-a-gun," Bertha said, half under her breath,

and put the keys back in the ignition.

Frank Sellers sat there for as much as thirty seconds without saying a word. Then he pressed his foot on the starter button, slammed the car into gear, and made a U turn in the middle of the block. The siren started wailing again and the red spotlight blinked on and off.

We swung around the turn from Garden Vista Boulevard into Mantica Street and the broken-nosed cab driver was still at the wheel of his car.

Sellers braked the car to a stop alongside the taxi driver.

Shifty little eyes glittered out from either side of the broken nose.

"What's eating yuh?" the cab driver asked.

Sellers said, "Yesterday afternoon there was a smashup on Mantica Street and Garden Vista Boulevard. Know anything about it?"

"I heard it."

"Pick up a fare right afterward?"

Broken-nose frowned, then said, "Yes. What's it to you?"

"Man or woman?"

"Woman."

"What did she want?"

The glittering little eyes met Sellers's for a moment, then shifted.

Sellers suddenly threw open the door of the car, walked around, and stood with his broad shoulders hulking against the side of the taxicab. He whipped open the door of the cab. "Come out of that," he said to the driver.

Broken-nose sized him up, hesitated.

Sellers's hand shot forward, took a good grip on the necktie and shirt of the cab driver. He gave a jerk. "I said come out!"

The cab driver came out and was suddenly respectful. "What is it you want?" he asked.

"Your fare. What about it? Who was it?"

"A woman," he said. "She wanted me to shadow a

couple of cars that she said would be coming around the corner."

"Keep talking," Sellers said.

"When the car came around the corner on Mantica Street, we followed along. Then I noticed a second car was tagging after the first. I told my fare about it. She said never mind the second car, to stay with the first one. It was only about three blocks. They stopped down here at an apartment house. A man went in. The woman in the other car drove away. My fare told me to wait. We waited for about ten minutes."

"Go ahead."

"Then a jane came out of the apartment, jumped in a car, and drove away. My fare got excited. She got out, handed me a five-dollar bill, and said, 'That's for security on the fare.' She walked into the apartment house and was gone about ten minutes in all. Then she came back, got in the cab, and said, 'Drive to the Rimley Rendezvous.'

"We drove up to the Rimley Rendezvous. Some bastard had parked a car where it took up most of the cab space. I said, 'Wait a minute and I'll bust this car out of here!' But she didn't wait. She got out. She had to walk clean around the parked car. She walked around it and on into the Rimley Rendezvous. A guy came out and climbed into the parked car. I tried to shake him down for a buck. He wouldn't shake. I had five bucks for a sixty-cent ride, so I let him pull the old stall about having been shoved ahead into the cab space."

"Notice anything peculiar about this woman's handbag?" Sellers asked.

The cabbie looked at him with a certain dawning respect in his eyes. "She had something pretty heavy in her handbag. It stuck out. I thought it might have been—"

"A rod?" Sellers asked as the man hesitated.

"Uh huh. Only it wasn't a rod."

"Perhaps a hammer or a small hand ax?"

Sudden realization showed in the little eyes. "Hell,"

the cabbie said disgustedly, "that's what it was—and me wondering if it was a rod!"

"What did this woman look like?" Sellers asked.

"Not bad-looking," the driver said appreciatively. "Nice legs, swell hips, nice complexion. Teeth a little too big, that's all. Horse-toothed when she smiled."

"Fry me for an oyster!" Bertha exclaimed under her breath.

Chapter Nineteen

THE CASE IS CLOSED

ELLERY CRAIL WAS PACING BACK AND FORTH in front of our office when Bertha and I came up in the elevator.

His face lit with relief when he saw us. He came running forward and gripped my hand. "I was hoping you'd be here," he said. "The elevator operator said you folks frequently came in at night, although you didn't keep the office open after five o'clock."

Bertha said belligerently, "Well, we got you a settlement, and—"

"Let's go inside where we can talk," Crail said.

Bertha latchkeyed the door and we went into the private office.

Bertha went on, "Just like I told you over the telephone. You owe us three hundred dollars more and—"

Crail looked at her as though she might have been talking a foreign language, then he looked at me.

I shook my head and said, "I didn't tell her anything."

"What the hell are you two talking about?" Bertha asked.

Crail took a checkbook from his pocket, pulled out a fountain pen.

"Three hundred dollars," Bertha said.

Crail looked up at her and said, "Mrs. Cool, I want to thank you people for the most wonderful thing that has ever happened to me, and I think I owe every bit of my happiness to Donald Lam."

Bertha's jaw dropped.

Crail said, "I guess you know what happened—Lam seems to, anyway. I was suspicious of my wife and Stanberry. I wondered why she was so eager to have me buy the Stanberry Building at a price that my banker said was about three times too high. When she went out yesterday afternoon I—well, I decided to follow her. It was a decision I reached all at once. My car wasn't there, but I knew that it would be all right with Georgia Rushe if I borrowed her car. I borrowed it.

"I'm not going to tell you all that happened. Lam knows, anyway. I followed my wife. I saw the accident. I saw enough to know that she was deliberately following Stanberry. I went back to the office. Georgia didn't even know I'd borrowed her car—and then I read about Stanberry being murdered and—well, I put it up to my wife.

"She admitted that Stanberry had been blackmailing her. She wouldn't tell me what it was about. Well, you know—I wanted to be a strong, silent man. I wanted to be an understanding husband. I didn't ask any questions. I decided to back my wife to the limit. I knew that she'd be called as a witness in that automobile accident. I decided to have the case settled so that it could never be shown that her car was trailing Stanberry's. I came to you to get the case settled.

"And then Lam showed me how life can't be lived that way. You can't sacrifice yourself to keep from hurting someone if by doing so you're hurting someone else a great deal more. And—well, I had a talk with her, and this time I wasn't just a big sucker. I had in the back of my mind the knowledge of Georgia lying unconscious in a hospital, knowing that she had tried to take her life because of me, and I saw a lot of things in a slightly different light. And then Irma started talking about property settlement and was quite businesslike about the whole thing, and I realized that I'd been trapped into marriage simply as a financial investment. I was never so relieved in my life. I gave her a settlement that made her eyes bulge out and told her to get reservations for Reno, and came up here to find Donald Lam."

Crail took a deep breath and started writing on the check. He picked up a piece of blotting paper, blotted the check, tore it out, and tossed it on the desk. He got up and looked at me and there were tears in his eyes. He pushed out his hand and shook hands. Then he walked around the desk and hugged Bertha, leaned over and kissed her on the lips.

I said, "I'm glad you had your showdown, Crail. Your wife didn't murder Stanberry. It was another woman Stanberry had been blackmailing over the telephone. And if she hadn't noticed Stanberry's wrist watch was an hour fast and set it back the whole case might have been simplified—which doesn't mean your wife wasn't playing you for a sucker. She was.

"Esther Witson was being blackmailed and was tired of it. She followed Stanberry from the Rimley Rendezvous, determined to have a showdown. She may even have contemplated murder. She saw Stanberry go to this apartment house. She knew Billy Prue lived there. She put two and two together and waited. Then Billy Prue came out. Stanberry didn't. That made Miss Witson decide to investigate. She went up to Billy Prue's apartment. The door was open. She went in and saw a wonderful opportunity to get free of Stanberry once and for all. There was a note in his hand saying Billy had gone to a drugstore. She knew that was a lie. She'd seen Billy drive off, paying no attention to the drugstore on the corner. She saw a wonderful opportunity to free herself of Stanberry once and for all. She looked around for a weapon, found a hand ax, and hit Stanberry on the head once, hard. Then she got frightened and in a panic wanted to conceal the murder weapon. She sawed off some of the handle so it would fit into her purse, then ditched it in the first car she came to when she got out of the cab. The police found the short piece she'd sawed off the handle still in her purse."

Crail listened attentively. "Miss Witson, eh? I was afraid she'd bring my wife into it. And I was afraid someone might—oh, well, that's all finished now. I want to get back to the hospital. Good-by and bless you both. I've tried to express some of my gratitude in that check. You'll never know how deeply I am indebted to you."

Bertha watched him out the door, then grabbed up the check. I saw her greedy little eyes get big and round. "Fry me for an oyster!" she said in an awed voice. "Can me for a sardine!"

I was halfway across the outer office before Bertha came down to earth.

I heard her scream at me. "Goddamn you, Donald Lam! If you're headed for the Rimley Rendezvous, remember you can't charge any more cigarettes on the expense account. The case is closed."

I paused with my hand on the door. I couldn't resist a parting shot. "And if I'm not home tonight, don't worry about it," I said.

I whipped the door shut before Bertha could think of the answer to that one.

there was something dreadful in

the yellow room

When lovely Carol Spencer arrived to re-open the family summer mansion, she was frightened by a strange odor of fire that lingered in the empty rooms.

She traced it to a closed closet door, where it mingled with the smell of kerosene, burned paint—and something else. From that day on Carol would never forget the special terror behind that door.

A great mystery novel by
MARY ROBERTS RINEHART

the yellow room

A DELL BOOK   FORTY CENTS